The Alien

Raymond F. Jones

CONTENTS

THE COLONISTS

This was the rainy year. Last year had been the dry one, and it would come again. But they wouldn't be here to see it, Captain Louis Carnahan thought. They had seen four dry ones, and now had come the fourth wet one, and soon they would be going home. For them, this was the end of the cycle.

At first they had kept track of the days, checking each one off on their calendars, but the calendars had long since been mingled indistinguishably with the stuff of the planet itself—along with most of the rest of their equipment. By that time, however, they had learned that the cycle of wet and dry seasons was almost precisely equivalent to a pair of their own Terran years, so they had no more need for the calendars.

But at the beginning of this wet season Carnahan had begun marking off the days once again with scratches on the post of the hut in which he lived. The chronometers were gone, too, but one and three-quarters Earth days equalled one Serrengian day, and by that he could compute when the ships from Earth were due.

He had dug moats about the hut to keep rain water from coming in over his dirt floor. Only two of the walls were erected, and he didn't know or much care whether he would get the other two up or not. Most of the materials had blown away during the last dry period and he doubted very much that he would replace them. The two available walls were cornered against the prevailing winds. The roof was still in good shape, allowing him a sufficient space free of leaks to accommodate his cooking and the mat which he called a bed.

He picked up a gourd container from the rough bench in the center of the room and took a swallow of the burning liquid. From the front of the hut he looked out over the rain swept terrain at the circle of huts. Diametrically across from him he could see Bolinger, the little biologist, moving energetically about. Bolinger was the only one who had retained any semblance of scientific interest. He puttered continually over his collection, which had grown enormously over the eight year period.

When they got back, Bolinger at least would have some accomplishment to view with pride. The rest of them—?

Carnahan laughed sharply and took another big swallow from the gourd, feeling the fresh surge of hot liquor already crossing the portals of his brain, bringing its false sense of wisdom and clarity. He knew it was false, but it was the only source of wisdom he had left, he told himself.

He staggered back to the bed with the gourd. He caught a glimpse of his image in the small steel mirror on the little table at the end of the bed. Pausing to stare, he stroked the thick mat of beard and ran his fingers through the mane of hair that had been very black when he came, and was now a dirty silver grey.

He hadn't looked at himself for a long time, but now he had to. He had to know what they would see when the ships of Earth came to pick up the personnel of the Base and leave another crew. The image made him sick.

At the beginning of this final season of the rains, all his life before coming to Serrengia seemed like a dream that had never been real. Now it was coming back, as if he were measuring the final distance of a circle and approaching once again his starting point. He kept remembering more and more. Watching his image in the mirror, he remembered what General Winthrop had said on the day of their departure. "The pick of Earth's finest," the General said. "We have combed the Earth and you are the men we have chosen to represent Mankind in the far reaches of the Universe. Remember that wherever you go, there goes the honor of Mankind. Do not, above all, betray that honor."

Carnahan clenched his teeth in bitterness. He wished old fatty Winthrop had come with them. Savagely he upended the gourd and flung it across the room. It meant a trip to Bailey's hut to get it replenished. Bailey had been the Chief Physicist. Now he was the official distiller, and the rotgut he produced was the only thing that made existence bearable.

The Captain stared again at his own image. "Captain Louis Carnahan," he murmured aloud. "The pick of Earth's finest—!" He smashed a fist at the little metal mirror and sent it flying across the room. The table crashed over, one feeble leg twisting brokenly. Then Carnahan hunched over with his face buried against the bed. His fists beat against it while his shoulders jerked in familiar, drunken sobs.

After it was over he raised up, sitting on the edge of the bed. His mind burned with devastating clarity. It seemed for once he could remember everything that had ever happened to him. He remembered it all. He remembered his childhood under the bright, pleasant sky of Earth. He remembered his ambition to be a soldier, which meant spaceman, even then. He remembered his first flight, a simple training tour of the Moon installations. It convinced him that never again could he consider himself an Earthman in the sense of one who dwells upon the Earth. His realm was the sky and the stars. Not even the short period when he had allowed himself to be in love had changed his convictions. He had sacrificed everything his career demanded.

Where had it gone wrong? How could he have allowed himself to forget? For years he had forgotten, he realized in horror. He had forgotten that Earth existed. He had forgotten how he came to be here, and why. And all that he was meant to accomplish had gone undone. For years the scientific work of the great base expedition had been ignored. Only the little biologist across the way, pecking at his tasks season after season, had accomplished anything.

And now the ships were coming to demand an accounting.

He groaned aloud as the vision became more terrible. He thought of that day when they had arrived at the inhospitable and uninhabited world of Serrengia. He could close his eyes and see it again—the four tall ships standing on the plateau that was scarred by their landing. The men had been so proud of what they had done and would yet do. They could see nothing to defeat them as they unloaded the mountains of equipment and supplies.

Now that same equipment lay oozing in the muck of leafy decomposition, corroded and useless like the men themselves.

And in the dry seasons it had been alternately buried and blasted by the sands and the winds.

He remembered exactly the day and the hour when they had cracked beyond all recovery. With an iron hand he had held them for three years. Weekly he demanded an appearance in full dress uniform, and hard discipline in all their relationships was the rule. Then one day he let the dress review go. They had come in from a long trek through a jungle that was renewing itself after a dry season. Too exhausted in body and spirit, and filled with an increasing sense of futility, he abandoned for the moment the formalities he had held to.

After that it was easy. They fell apart all around him. He tried to hold them, settling quarrels that verged on mutiny. Then in the sixth month of the fourth year he had to kill with his own hands the first of his crazed and rebellious crew. The scientific work disintegrated and was abandoned. He remembered he had locked up all their notes and observations and charts, but where he had hidden the metal chest was one of the few things he seemed unable to recall.

The more violent of the expedition killed each other off, or wandered into the jungle or desert and never came back. On the even dozen who were left there had settled a kind of monastic hermitage. Each man kept to himself, aware that a hairbreadth trespass against his neighbor would mean quick challenge to the death. Yet they clung to membership in this degenerate community as if it represented their last claim to humanness.

This is what they would see though. They would see his personal failure. It was his, there was no question of that. If he had been strong he could have held the expedition together. He could have maintained the base in all the strength and honor of military tradition that had been entrusted to him. He hadn't been strong enough.

The ships would come. The four of them. They might come tomorrow or even today. A panic crept through him. The ships could land at any time now, and their men would come marching out to greet him in his failure and cowardice and his dishonor. It must not happen. Old fatty Winthrop had said one thing that made sense: "—there goes the honor of Mankind. Do not, above all, betray that honor."

Fatty was right. The only thing he had left was honor, and in only one way could he retain it.

With the fiery clarity burning in his brain he struggled from where he lay and picked up the metallic mirror and hung it from the post near the bed. He turned up the broken table against the wall. Then, with the air of one who has not been on the premises for a long time he began searching through the long unused chests stacked in the corner. The contents were for the most part in a state of decay, but he found his straight edged razor in the oiled pouch where he had last placed it.

There should have been shaving detergent, but he couldn't find it. He contented himself with preparing hot water, then slowly and painfully hacked the thick beard away and scraped his face clean. He found a comb and raked it through his tangled mat of hair, arranging it in some vague resemblance to the cut he used to wear.

From the chests he drew forth the dress uniform he had put away so long ago. Fortunately, it had been in the center, surrounded by other articles so that it was among the best preserved of his possessions. He donned it in place of the rags he wore. The shoes were almost completely hard from lack of care, but he put them on anyway and brushed the toes with a scrap of cloth.

From underneath his bed he took his one possession which he had kept in meticulous repair, his service pistol. Then he stood up, buttoning and smoothing his coat, and smiled at himself in the little mirror. But his gaze shifted at once to something an infinity away.

"'Do not, above all, betray that honor.' At least you gave us one good piece of advice, fatty," he said.

Carefully, he raised the pistol to his head.

Hull number four was erect and self-supporting. Its shell enclosure was complete except for necessary installation openings. And in Number One the installations were complete and the ship's first test flight was scheduled for tomorrow morning.

John Ashby looked from the third story window of his office toward the distant assembly yards on the other side of the field. The four hulls stood like golden flames in the afternoon sunlight. Ashby felt defeated by the speed with which the ships were being completed. It was almost as if the engineers had a special animosity toward him, which they expressed in their unreasonable speed of construction. This was nonsense, of course. They had a job to do and were proud if they could cut time from their schedule.

But there was no cutting time from his schedule, and without the completion of his work the ships would not fly. He had to find men capable of taking them on their fantastic journeys. To date, he had failed.

He glanced down at the black car with government markings, which had driven in front of the building a few moments before, and then he heard Miss Haslam, his secretary, on the interphone. "The Colonization Commission, Dr. Ashby."

He turned from the window. "Have them come in at once," he said.

He strode to the door and shook hands with each of the men. Only four of them had come: Mr. Merton, Chairman; General Winthrop; Dr. Cowper; and Dr. Boxman.

"Please have seats over here by the window," Ashby suggested.

They accepted and General Winthrop stood a moment looking out. "A beautiful sight, aren't they, Ashby?" he said. "They get more beautiful every day. You ought to get over more often. Collins says you haven't been around the place for weeks, and Number One is going up tomorrow."

"We've had too much to occupy us here."

"My men are ready," said the General pointedly. "We could supply a dozen crews to take those ships to Serrengia and back, and man the base there."

Ashby turned away, ignoring the General's comment. He took a chair at the small conference table where the three Commissioners had seated themselves. Winthrop followed, settling in his chair with a smile, as if he had scored a major point.

"Number One is ready," said Merton, "and still you have failed to offer us a single man, Dr. Ashby. The Commission feels that the time is very near when definite action will have to be taken. We have your reports, but we wanted a personal word with you to see if we couldn't come to some understanding as to what we can expect."

"I will send you the men when I find out what kind of man we need," said Ashby. "Until then there had better be no thought of releasing the colonization fleet. I will not be responsible for any but the right answers to this problem."

"We are getting to the point," said Boxman, "where we feel forced to consider the recommendations of General Winthrop. Frankly, we have never been able to fully understand your objections."

"There'll never be a time when I cannot supply all the men needed to establish this base," said Winthrop. "We spend unlimited funds and years of time training personnel for posts of this kind, yet you insist on looking for unprepared amateurs. It makes no sense whatever, and only because you have been given complete charge of the personnel program have you been able to force your views on the Commission. But no one understands you. In view of your continued failure, the Commission is going to be forced to make its own choice."

"My resignation may be had at any time," said Ashby.

"No, no, Dr. Ashby." Merton held up his hand. "The General is perhaps too impulsive in his disappointment that you have failed us so far, but we do not ask for your resignation. We do ask if there is not some way in which you might see fit to use the General's men in manning the base."

"The whole answer lies in the erroneous term you persist in applying to this project," said Ashby. "It is not a base, and never will be. We propose to set up a colony. It makes an enormous difference with respect to the kind of men required. We've been over this before—"

"But not enough," snapped Winthrop. "We'll continue to go over it until you understand you can't waste those ships on a bunch of half-baked idealists inspired by some noble nonsense about carrying on the torch of human civilization beyond the stars. We're putting up a base, to gather scientific data and establish rights of occupancy."

"I don't think I agree with your description of my proposed party of colonists," said Ashby mildly.

"That's what they'll be! Were colonists ever anything but psalm singing rebels or cutthroats trying to escape hanging? You're not going to establish a cultural and scientific base with such people."

"No, you're quite right. That's not the kind."

"What is it you're looking for?" said Merton irritably. "What kind of men do you want, if you can't find them among the best and the worst humanity offers."

"Your terms are hardly accurate," said Ashby. "You fail to recognize the fact that we have never known what kind of man it takes to colonize. You ignore the fact that we have never yet successfully colonized the planets of our own Solar System. Bases, yes—but all our colonies have failed to date."

"What better evidence could you ask for in support of my argument?" demanded Winthrop. "We've proved bases are practical, and that colonies are not."

"No matter how far away or how long the periods of rotation, a man assigned to a base expects to return home. Night or day, in the performance of any duty, there is in his mind as a working background the recognition that at some future time he can go home. His base is never his home."

"Precisely. That is what makes the base successful."

Ashby shook his head. "No base is ever successful from the standpoint of permanent extension of a civilization. By its very nature it is transitory, impermanent. That is not what we want now."

"We have the concept of permanent bases in military thinking," said Winthrop. "You can't generalize in that fashion."

"Name for me a single military or expeditionary base that continued its permanency over any extended period of history."

"Well—now—"

"The concept is invalid," said Ashby. "Extensions of humanity from one area to another on a permanent basis are made by colonists. Men who do not expect to rotate, but come to live and establish homes. This is what we want on Serrengia. Humanity is preparing to make an extension of itself in the Universe.

"But more than this, there are limitations of time and distance in the establishment of bases, which cannot be overcome by any amount of training of personnel. Cycles of rotation and distances from home can be lengthened beyond the capacity of men to endure. It is only when they go out with no expectation of return that time and distance cease to control them."

"We do not know of any such limitations," said Winthrop. "They have not been met here in the Solar System."

"We know them," said Ashby. "The thing we have not found and which we must discover before those ships depart is the quality that makes it possible for a man to ignore time and distance and his homeland. We know a good deal about the successful colonists of Earth's history. We know that invariably they were of some minority group which felt itself persecuted or limited by conditions surrounding it, or else they were fleeing the results of some crime."

"If that is what you are looking for, it is no wonder you have failed," said Dr. Cowper. "We have no such minority groups in our society."

"Very true," Ashby replied. "But it is not the condition of fleeing or being persecuted that generates the qualities of a perfect colonist by any means! We have examples enough of adequately persecuted groups who failed as colonists. But there is some quality, which seems to appear, if at all, only in some of those who have courage enough to flee their oppression or limiting conditions. This quality makes them successful in their colonization.

"We are looking first, therefore, for individuals who would have the courage to resist severe limitations to the extent of flight, if such limitations existed. And among these we hope to find the essence of that which makes it possible for a man to cut all ties with his homeland."

"So you are making your search," said Merton, "among the potentially rebellious and criminal?"

Ashby nodded. "We have confined our study to these individuals as a result of strict historical precedent so that we might narrow the search as much as possible. You must understand, however, that to choose merely the rebellious and staff our ships with these would be foolhardy. It would be a ridiculous shotgun technique. Some of them would succeed, but we would never know which it would be. We might send twenty or a thousand ships out and establish one successful colony.

"We have to do much better than that. Our consumption of facilities on this project is so great that we have to know, within a negligible margin of error, that when these groups are visited in eight or fifty years from now we will find a community of cooperative, progressive human beings. We cannot be satisfied with less!"

"I'm afraid the majority of sentiment in the Commission is not in agreement with you," said Mr. Merton. "To oppose General Winthrop's trained crews with selected cutthroats and traitors may have historical precedent, but it scarcely seems the optimum procedure in this case!

"We are willing to be shown proof of your thesis, Dr. Ashby, but we have certain realities of which we are sure. If we can do no better, we shall take the best available to us at the time the ships are ready. If you cannot supply us with proven crews and colonists by then we shall be forced to accept General Winthrop's recommendations and choose personnel whose reactions are at least known and predictable to a high degree. I'm sorry, but surely you can understand our position in this matter."

For a long time Ashby was silent, looking from one to the other of the faces about the table. Then he spoke in a low voice, as if having reached the extremity of his resources. "Yes—the reactions of Winthrop's men are indeed known. I suggest that you come with me and I will show you what those reactions are."

He stood up and the others followed with inquiring expressions on their faces. Winthrop made a short, jerky motion of his head, as if he detected a hidden sting in Ashby's words. "What do you mean by that?" he demanded.

"You don't suppose that our examinations would neglect the men on whom you have spent so much time and effort in training?"

The General flushed with rage. "If you've tampered with any of my men—! You had no right—!"

The other Commission members were smiling in faint amusement at the General's discomfiture.

"I should think it would be to your advantage to check the results of your training," said Mr. Merton.

"There is only one possible check!" exclaimed General Winthrop. "Put these men on a base for a period of eight years and at a distance of forty seven light years from home and see what they will do. That is the only way you can check on them."

"And if you know anything about our methods of testing, you will understand that this, in effect, is what we have done. Your best man is about to be released from the test pit. He can't have more than an hour to go."

"Who have you got in your guinea pig pen?" the General demanded. "If you've ruined him—"

"Captain Louis Carnahan," said Ashby. "Shall we go down, gentlemen?"

It had been a grisly business, watching the final minutes of Carnahan's disintegration. General Winthrop's face was almost purple when he saw the test pit in which Carnahan was being examined. He tried to tear out the observation lens with his bare hands as he saw the Captain lift the loaded pistol to his head in the moment before the safety beam cut in.

And now Ashby kept hearing Winthrop's furious, scathing voice: "You have destroyed one of the best men the Service has ever produced! I'll have your hide for this, Ashby, if it's the last act of my life."

Merton and the others had been shocked also by the violence and degradation of what they saw, but whether he had made his point or not, Ashby didn't know. Carnahan, of course, would be returned to the Service within twenty four hours, all adverse effects of the test completely removed. He would be aware that he had taken it and had not passed, but there would be no trace of the bitter emotions generated during those days of examination.

Ashby looked out again at the four hulls now turning from gold to red as the sun dropped lower in the sky. He had not asked Merton if the ultimatum was going to stick. He wondered how they could insist on it after what they had seen, but he didn't know.

Impatiently, he turned from the window as Miss Haslam's voice came on the intercom once more. "Dr. Ashby, Mr. Jorden is still waiting to see you."

Jorden. He had forgotten. The man had been waiting during his conference with the Commissioners. Jorden was the one who had been rejected for examination two weeks ago and insisted he had a right to be examined for colonization factors. He had been trying to get in ever since. He might as well get rid of the man once and for all, Ashby decided reluctantly.

"Show him in," he said.

Mark Jorden was a tall, blond man in his late twenties. Shaking hands with him, Ashby felt thick, strong fingers and glimpsed a massive wrist at the edge of the coat sleeve. Jorden's face was a pleasant Scandinavian pink, matched by blue eyes that looked intently into Ashby's face.

They sat at the desk. "You want to be a colonist," said Ashby. "You say you want to settle forty seven light years from Earth for the rest of your life. And our preliminary psycho tests indicate you have scarcely a vestige of the basic qualities required. Why do you insist on the full examination?"

Jorden smiled and shook his head honestly. "I don't know exactly. It seems like something I'd enjoy doing. Maybe it's in my people—they liked to move around and see new places. They were seamen in the days when there weren't any charts to sail by."

"It's certain that this is a situation without charts to sail by," said Ashby, "but I hardly think the word 'enjoy' is applicable. Have you thought at all of what existence means at that distance from Earth, with no communication whatever except a ship every eight years or so? Qualifications just a trifle short of insanity are required for a venture of that kind."

"I'm sure you don't mean that, Dr. Ashby," said Jorden reprovingly.

"Perhaps not," said Ashby. His visitor's calm assurance irritated him, as if he were the one who knew what a colonist ought to be. "I see by your application you're an electrical engineer."

Jorden nodded. "Yes. My company has just offered me the head of the department, but I had to explain I was putting in an application for colonist. They think I'm crazy, of course."

"Does taking the examination mean giving up your promotion?"

17

"I'm not sure. But I rather think they will pass me up and give it to one of the other men."

"You want to go badly enough to risk giving up that chance in order to take an examination which will unquestionably show you have no qualifications whatever to be a colonist?"

"I think I'm qualified," said Jorden. "I insist on being given the chance. I believe I have the right to it."

Ashby tried to restrain his irritation. What Jorden said was perhaps true. No one had ever raised the point before. Those previously rejected by the preliminary tests had withdrawn in good grace. It seemed senseless to waste the time of a test pit and its large crew on an obviously hopeless applicant. On the other hand, he couldn't afford to have Jorden stirring up trouble with the Colonization Commission at this critical time—and he could guess that was exactly what Jorden's next move would be if he were turned down again.

"Our machines will find out everything about you later," said Ashby, "but I'd like you to tell me about yourself so that I may feel personally acquainted with you."

Jorden shrugged. "There's not much to tell. I had the usual schooling, which wasn't anything impressive. I had my three year hitch in the Service, and I suppose that's where I began to feel there was something available in life which I had never anticipated. I suppose it sounds very silly to you, but when I first put a foot on the Moon I felt like crying. I picked up a handful of pumice and let it sift through my fingers. I looked out toward Mars and felt as if I could go anywhere, that I ought to go everywhere.

"The medicos told me later that it was a crazy sort of feeling that everyone gets his first time out, but I didn't believe them. I didn't believe it was quite the same with anyone else. When I got out to Mars finally, and during my one tour on Pluto, it seemed to get worse instead of decreasing as they told me it would. When I got out I took a job in my profession, and I've been satisfied, but I've never been able to get rid of the feeling there's something I'm missing, something I ought to be doing. It's connected with everything out there." He lifted a broad hand and gestured to the horizon beyond the windows.

"Perhaps your career should have been in the Service," suggested Ashby.

"No. That was good enough while it lasted, but they didn't have anything I wanted permanently. When I heard about the proposed colonization on Serrengia that seemed to be it."

"Your application indicates you are not married."

"That's right," said Jorden. "I have no ties to hold me back."

"You understand, of course, that as a colonist you will be expected to marry, either before leaving or soon after arrival. Colonial life is family life."

"I hadn't thought much about that, but it can't be too bad, I suppose. I presume my choice would be quite severely limited to a fellow colonist?"

"Correct."

"There is a story about my third or fourth grandfather who was given a girl to marry the night before he sailed from his homeland to settle in a new country. They had seventeen children and were said to be extraordinarily happy. My family still owns the homestead they cleared. I was born there."

"It can be done, but it doesn't conform closely with our currently accepted social mores," said Ashby hopefully.

"I'm sure that won't stand in my way. If there's a woman who's willing to take a chance, I certainly will be."

"There's one more thing we have to know," said Ashby. "What are you running away from? Who or what are your enemies?"

Jorden laughed uncertainly. "I'm sorry, but I'm not running away from anything. As far as I know I have no enemies."

"All colonists are running from something," said Ashby. "Otherwise they would stay where they are."

Jorden regarded him a moment in silence, then smiled slowly. "I think you are going to have occasion to revise that thesis," he said.

"A great deal of history would also have to be revised if we did," said Ashby. "At any rate, let's go down to the test pits. I'll show you what's in store for you there, and you can further decide if you insist on going through with it."

The laboratories of the Institute of Social Science were spread over a forty acre area, consisting mostly of the test pits where experimental examination of proposed colonists was being conducted. Ashby led his visitor to the ground floor where they took a pair of the electric cycles used for transportation along the vast corridors of the laboratory.

A quarter of a mile away they stopped and entered a glassed-in control room fitted with a number of desks and extensive banks of electronic equipment.

"This almost looks like a good sized computer setup," said Jorden admiringly.

"We use computers extensively, but this equipment is merely the recording and control apparatus for the synthetic environment established in the test pit. Please step this way."

The control room was empty now, but during a test it was occupied by a dozen technicians. It was a highly unorthodox procedure to show a prospective colonist the test pit setup before examination, but Ashby still had hopes of shunting Jorden aside without wasting the facilities on a useless test.

They moved to an observation post and Ashby directed Jorden's attention to the observation lenses. "We cleaned out here this afternoon," he said. "A Captain of the Service last occupied the pit."

Jorden looked up inquiringly. "Did he—?"

"No. He didn't make it. Tomorrow morning you will be given a preconditioning which will set up the basic situation that you have traveled to Serrengia and are now established there in the colony. We will begin the test at a period of some length after establishment there, when difficulties begin to pile up. Other members of the party will be laboratory staff people who will provide specific, guiding stimuli to determine your reaction to them."

"Are they there constantly, night and day?"

"No. When you are asleep their day's work is over and they go home."

"What if I wake up and find the whole setup is a phony?"

"You won't. We have control beams constantly focussed upon the persons being tested. These are used to keep him asleep when desirable, and to control him to the extent of preventing him doing physical harm to himself or others."

"Is that necessary?" said Jorden dubiously. "Why should anyone wish to do harm?"

"The Captain, whom we released today, was pushed to the point of suicide," said Ashby. "We find it quite necessary to assure ourselves of adequate control at all times."

"How can you set up the illusion of distance and a whole new world in such a comparatively small area?"

"It is illusion, a great deal of it. Some is induced along with the initial preconditioning, other features are done mechanically, but when you are there you will have no doubt whatever that you are a colonist on the planet Serrengia. You will act accordingly, and respond to the stimuli exactly as if you had been transported to the actual planet. In this way, we are sure of finding colonists who will not blow up when they face the real situation."

"How many have you found so far?"

"None."

Jorden was shaken for a moment, but he smiled then and said, "You have found one. Put my name down on the books."

"We'll see," said Ashby grimly. "Your colony will be in the limited belt of the planet's northern hemisphere where considerable agriculture is possible. You'll be in the midst of a group trying to beat a living from a world which is neither excessively hostile nor conducive to indolence. Some of the people will be bitter and wish they had never come. They will break up in groups and fight each other. They will challenge every reason you have for your own coming. You will face your own personal impoverishment, the death of your child—"

"Child?" said Jorden.

"Yes. You will be provided with a wife and three children. One of these will die, and you will react as if it were your own flesh. Your wife will oppose your staying, and demand a return to Earth. We will throw at you every force available to tear down your determination to build a colony. We shall test in every possible way the validity of your decision to go. Do you still wish to go through with it?"

Jorden's grin was somewhat fainter. He took a deep breath as he nodded slowly. "Yes, I'll go through with it. I think it's what I want."

When Ashby finally returned alone to the office, Miss Haslam had gone home. He put in a call anyway for Dr. Bonnie Nathan. She usually remained somewhere in the laboratory until quite late, even when not assigned to a test.

In a few minutes her voice came over the phone. "John? What can I do for you?"

"I thought I could let you off for a few days," said Ashby, "but we've got another one that's come up rather suddenly." He told her briefly about Mark Jorden. "It's useless, but I don't want him running to the Commission right now, so we'll put him through. You'll be the wife. We'll use Program Sixty Eight, except that we'll accelerate it."

"Accelerate—!"

"Yes. It won't hurt him any. Whatever happens we can wipe up afterwards. This is simply a nuisance and I want it out of the way as quickly as possible. After that—perhaps I can give you those few days I promised you. O.K.?"

"It's all right with me," said Bonnie. "But an accelerated Sixty Eight—"

They stood on a low hillock overlooking the ninety acres of bottom land salvaged from the creek grass. Mark Jorden shaded his eyes and squinted critically over the even stand of green shoots emerging from the bronzed soil. Germination had been good in spite of the poor planting time. The chance of getting a crop out was fair. If they didn't they'd be eating shoe plastic in another few months.

The ten year old boy beside him clutched his hand and edged closer as if there were something threatening him from the broad fields. "Isn't there any way at all for Earth to send us food," he said, "if we don't get a crop?"

"We have to make believe Earth doesn't exist, Roddy," said Jorden. "We couldn't even let them know we need help, we're so far away." He gripped the boy's shoulders solidly in his big hands and drew him close. "We aren't going to need any help from Earth. We're going to make it on our own. After all, what would they do on Earth if they couldn't make it? Where would they go for outside help?"

"I know," said the boy, "but there are so many of them they can't fail. Here, there's only the few of us."

Jorden patted his shoulder gently again as they started moving toward the rough houses a half mile away. "That makes it all the easier for us," he said. "We don't have to worry about the ones who won't cooperate. We can't lose with the setup we've got."

It was harder for Roddy. He remembered Earth, although he had been only four when they left. He still remembered the cities and the oceans and the forests he had known so briefly, and was cursed with the human nostalgia for a past that seemed more desirable than an unknown, fearful future.

Of the other children, Alice had been a baby when they left, and Jerry had been born during the trip. They knew only Serrengia and loved its wild, uncompromising rigor. They spent their abandoned wildness of childhood in the nearby hills and forests. But with Roddy it was different. Childhood seemed to have slipped by him. He was moody, and moved carefully in constant fear of this world he would never willingly call home. Jorden's heart ached with longing to instill some kind of joy into him.

"That looks like Mr. Tibbets," said Roddy suddenly, his eyes on the new log house.

"I believe you're right," said Jorden. "It looks like Roberts and Adamson with him. Quite a delegation. I wonder what they want."

The colony consisted of about a hundred families, each averaging five members. Originally they had settled on a broad plateau at some distance from the river. It was a good location overlooking hundreds of miles of desert and forest land. Its soil was fertile and the river water was lifted easily through the abundant power of the community atomic energy plant which had been brought from Earth.

Three months ago, however, the power plant had been destroyed in a disastrous explosion that killed almost a score of the colonists. Crops for their next season's food supply were half matured and could not be saved by any means available.

The community was broken into a number of smaller groups. Three of these, composed of fifteen families each, moved to the low lands along the river bank and cleared acreage for new crops in a desperate hope of getting a harvest before the season ended. They had not yet learned enough of the cycle of weather in this area to predict it with much accuracy.

Mark Jorden was in charge of one of the farms and the elected leader of the village in which he lived.

Tibbets was an elderly man from the same village. In his middle sixties, he presented a puzzle to Jorden as to why he had been permitted to come. Roberts and Adamson were from the settlements farther down the river.

Jorden felt certain of the reason for their visit. He didn't want to hear what they had to say, but he knew he might as well get it over with.

They hailed him from the narrow wooden porch. Jorden came up the steps and shook hands with each. "Won't you come in? I'm sure Bonnie can find something cool to drink."

Tibbets wiped his thin, wrinkled brow. "She already has. That girl of yours doesn't waste any time being told what to do. It's too bad some of the others can't pitch in the way Bonnie does."

Jorden accepted the praise without comment, wondering if no one else at all were aware of the hot, violent protests she sometimes poured out against him because of the colony.

"Come in anyway," Jorden said. "I have to go back to the watering in a little while, but you can take it easy till then." He led the way into the log house.

Their homes on the plateau had been decent ones. With adequate power they had made lumber and cement, and within a year of their landing had built a town of fine homes. Among those who had been forced to abandon them, no one was more bitter than Bonnie. "You're no farmer," she said. "Why can't those who are be the ones to move?"

Now, when he came into the kitchen, she was tired, but she tried to smile as always at her pleasure in seeing him again. He couldn't imagine what it would be like not having her to welcome him from the fields.

"I'll get something cool for you and Roddy," she said. "Would you gentlemen like another drink?"

When they were settled in the front room Tibbets spoke. "You know why we've come, Mark. The election is only a couple of months away. We can't have Boggs in for another term of governor. You've got to say you'll run against him."

"As I told you last time, Boggs may be a poor excuse for the job, but I'd be worse. He's at least an administrator. I'm only an engineer—and more recently a farmer."

"We've got something new, now," said Tibbets, his eyes suddenly cold and meaningful.

"The talk about his deliberately blowing up the power plant? Talk of that kind could blow up the whole colony as well. Boggs may have his faults but he's not insane."

"We've got proof now," said Tibbets. "It's true. Adamson's got the evidence. He got one of the engineers who escaped the blast to talk. It's one of them who were supposed to have been killed. He's so scared of Boggs he's still hiding out. But he's got the proof and those who are helping him know it's true."

"Tibbets is right," said Adamson earnestly. "We know it's true. And something like that can't stay hidden. It's got to be brought out if we're going to make the colony survive. You can't just shut your eyes to it and say, 'Good old Boggs would never do a thing like that.'"

Jorden's eyes were darker as he spoke in low tones now, hoping Roddy would not be listening in the kitchen. "Suppose it is true. Why would Boggs do such an insane thing?"

"Because he's an insane man," said Tibbets. "That's the obvious answer. He wants to destroy the colony and limit its growth. He was satisfied to come here and be elected governor and run the show. He saw it as means of becoming a two-bit dictator over a group of subservient colonists. It hasn't turned out that way. He found a large percentage of engineers and scientists who would have none of his nonsense.

"He saw the group becoming something bigger than himself. He had to cut it down to his own size. He's willing to destroy what he can't possess, but he believes that by reducing us to primitive status he can keep us in line. In either case the colony loses."

"If what you say is true—if it's actually true," Jorden said, his eyes suddenly far away, "we've got to fight him—"

"Then we can count on you?"

"Yes—you can count on me."

He stood in the doorway watching the departure of the three men, but he was aware of Bonnie behind him. She rushed to him as he turned, and put her face against his chest.

"Mark—you can't do it! Boggs will kill you. This is no concern of ours. We don't belong to Maintown any more. It's their business up there. I'd go crazy if anything happened to you. You've got to think of the rest of us!"

"I am thinking," said Mark. He raised her chin so he could look into her eyes. "I'm thinking that we are going to live here the rest of our lives, and so are the children. If the story about Boggs is true, we're all concerned. We wouldn't be down here if the power plant hadn't been destroyed. We'd be living in our good home in Maintown. Would you expect me to let Boggs get away with this without raising a hand to stop him?"

"Yes—I would," said Bonnie, "because there is nothing anyone can do. You know he has Maintown in the palm of his hand. He's screened out every ruffian and soured colonist in the whole group and they'll do anything he says. You can't fight them all, Mark. I won't let you."

"It won't be me alone," said Jorden. "If it develops into a fight the majority of the colony will be with us. Earth will be with us. Boggs will be facing the results of the whole two billion year struggle it took to make man what he now is."

In the lounge off the lab cafeteria, Ashby indulged in a late coffee knowing he wouldn't sleep anyway. Across the table Bonnie ate sparingly of a belated supper.

"The threat of having to fight Boggs didn't give him much of a scare," said Ashby thoughtfully.

"It'll take a lot more than a bogey man like Boggs to scare Mark," said Bonnie. "You've got yourself a bigger quantity of man than you bargained for."

"This might turn out to be more interesting than we thought. I wish there were more time to spend on him. But Merton called up again today to verify the ultimatum I told you about. We produce colonists by the time Hull Four is complete or they turn the personnel problem over to Winthrop—even after they saw Carnahan go to pieces before their eyes."

"Has it ever occurred to you," said Bonnie slowly, "that we might just possibly be off on the wrong foot? How do you know that any of the colonists of Earth's history could have stood up to the demands of Serrengia? I'm beginning to suspect that the Mayflower's passenger list would have folded quite completely under these conditions. They had it comparatively easy. So did most other successful colonists."

"Yes—?" said Ashby.

"Maybe they succeeded in spite of being rebels. If they could have come to the new lands without the pressure of flight, but in complete freedom of action, they might have made an even greater success."

"But why would they have come at all, then?"

"I don't know. There must be another motive capable of impelling them. In great feats of exploration, creation—other human actions similar to colonization—"

"There are no other human actions similar to colonization," said Ashby. "Surely you realize we're dealing with something unique here, Bonnie!"

"I know—all I'm trying to say is there could be another valid motive. I think Mark Jorden's got it. There's something different about this test, and I think you ought to look in on it yourself."

"What's so different about him?"

"He doesn't act like the rest. He hasn't any apparent reason for being here."

Ashby looked at the girl closely. She was one of his top staff members and had been with him from the beginning. The incredible strain of working day after day in the test pits was showing its effects, he thought.

"I shouldn't have let you get started on this one," he said. "You're fagged out. Maybe it would be better to erase what we've done and start over, so that you can drop out."

She shook her head with a quickness that surprised him. "I want to finish it, and see how Mark turns out. I'm so used to working with the bitter, anti-social ones that it's a relief to have someone who is halfway normal and gregarious. I want to be around when we find out why he's here."

"Especially if he should go all the way to the end. But he won't–"

Ashby was genuinely concerned about Bonnie's condition when he looked in on her the next morning. The strain on her face was real beyond any matter of make-up or acting. He wondered just why she should be giving in to it now. Bonnie was well trained, as were all the staff members who worked in the test pits. The emotional conflicts mocked up there were not allowed to penetrate very deeply into their personal experience, yet it looked now as if Bonnie had somehow lost control of the armor to protect against such invasion. She seemed to be living the circumstances of the test program almost as intensely as Mark Jorden was doing.

Such a condition couldn't be permitted to continue, but he was baffled by it. Her physical and emotional check prior to the test had not shown her threshold to be this low. Evidently there was emotional dynamite buried somewhere in the situation they had manufactured.

Through the observation lens of the test pit Ashby watched Jorden begin a tour of the villages, making a quiet investigation of the situation, which he had all but ignored until it was forced to his attention. Jorden spent an hour with Adamson, listening carefully to the atomic engineer's story, and then was led to the hiding place of the engineer who claimed direct evidence that Boggs had instigated the explosion at the power plant.

As Adamson left them, Ashby signaled him through the tiny button buried in the skin behind his right ear. "This is Ashby," he said. "How does it look? Do you think he's going to tackle Boggs?"

"No question of that." Adamson's words came back, although he made no movement of his mouth or throat. "Jorden is one of these people with a lot of inertia. It takes a big push to get him moving, but when he really gets rolling there isn't much that can stop him, either. You're really going to have to put the pressure on to find his cracking point."

"I'm afraid we're likely to find Bonnie's first. There's something about this that's hitting her too hard. Do you know what it is?"

"No," said Adamson. "I thought I noticed it a little yesterday, too. Maybe we ought to check her out."

"She insists on completing the program. And I'd like to go all the way with Jorden. I'm becoming rather curious about him. Keep an eye on Bonnie and let me know what you think at the end of the shift."

"I'll do that," said Adamson.

Jorden followed his guide for more than a mile beyond the last village on the bank of the river. There, in a willow hidden cave in the clay bank, he found James, the atomic engineer who was reported to know of Boggs' attack on the power plant.

"I told him you were coming," said Adamson, "but I'm going to leave. You can make out better if you're alone with him. He's bitter, but he isn't armed, and he'll go along with you if you don't push him too hard."

Jorden watched Adamson disappear along the bank in the direction from which they had come. He had a feeling of utter ridiculousness. This wasn't what they had come for! They had come to build an outpost of human beings, to establish man's claim in this sector of the Universe. And they were ending in a petty conflict worthy of the politics of centuries before, back on Earth.

His face took on a harder set as he approached the mouth of the cave and whistled the signal notes that Adamson had taught him. If the establishment of the colony demanded this kind of fight then he was willing to enter the battle. He had not dedicated the remainder of his life to a goal only to abandon it to a petty tyrant like Boggs.

A bearded face peered cautiously through parted willows and James' voice spoke. "You're Jorden? I suppose by now everybody in the villages knows where I'm hiding out. I'm the world's prize fool for letting this parade come past my place. Come in and I'll tell you what I know. If you help get Boggs it will be worth anything it costs me."

Jorden followed the man through the screening willows to the mouth of the cave. There the two of them squatted on rocks opposite each other.

"I remember you now," said James. "You set up the electric plant when we were assembling the pile, didn't you? I thought we'd worked together."

Jorden nodded, hoping James would go on, remembering Adamson's caution not to push him too hard, but the engineer seemed to have nothing more to say. He rubbed a hand forcibly against his other arm and looked beyond the mouth of the cave to the slow moving river.

"This business concerning Boggs' destruction of the plant—how did it start?" said Jorden finally.

"How does anything of that kind start?" said James. "Boggs came to some of us and remarked in casual conversation what a shame it would be if the colony were to duplicate all over again the mistakes that Earth have made during the past thousands of years. A few of us were sympathetic with that thought—it would indeed be a shame. Some of the engineers thought that this was the perfect chance to set up a truly scientific society. They didn't agree that Boggs was the ideal leader, but he was the leader and the obvious one to work through. They all became convinced that a rapid industrialization and a highly technological society built upon the old rusty foundations would be most difficult to overcome in building a society on truly adequate sociological principles. You can take it from there."

Yes, he could, Jorden thought. Anybody could take it from there.

It was the oldest lie that men of power and position had ever concocted. Why had those particular colonists fallen for it?

"What about you?" he asked James. "Were you sucked in by Boggs' arguments?"

The engineer nodded. "He took all of us. And all along he never intended that more than a couple would get out alive—by double crossing the others."

"Why?" said Jorden.

"Why? I've thought a lot about that, living here in this mudhole. You get to thinking about things like that when you realize there's no going back, that Boggs would kill me on sight for what I could tell—and that the other colonists would also, because of what I've done. Adamson says I can trust him. He says I can trust you. But I don't trust anybody. I know that someday soon I'm going to get a bullet in the head from one of you. All I'm hoping is that some of you hate Boggs enough to get him first."

"Why did you come to Serrengia in the first place?"

"To get away. Why did anyone come? You don't give up everything you've got in order to go to some strange world and spend the rest of your life unless you've got a reason. Unless you hate what you've got so much you're willing to try anything else. Unless you're so terribly afraid of what could happen to you back there that you're willing to face any kind of dangers out here. We all had our reasons. I'm not asking yours. It makes no difference to you what mine were. But they're all alike. We came because we were so afraid or full of hate we couldn't stay."

"How did you expect to build a new world out of hate and fear of the old one?"

"Who worried about what we'd build here? All we wanted to do was get away. You can't tell me you came for any other reason!"

Jorden made no answer. He continued to stare in wonder at the atomic engineer. To what extent were James' words actually true? How completely was the colony riddled with unpredictable, purposeless characters like him?

If they had fled Earth with a purpose to create something better than they left, there was a chance. But if James was right that most of them had come in blind flight with no goal at all then the Earth colony of Serrengia would be dead long before the ships came again.

But Jorden did not believe this. He did not believe that any but a small fraction of the colonists had any feeling toward Earth except that of love. Most had come because they wanted to do this particular thing with their lives. Nothing had driven or forced them to it.

"Tell me what Boggs did, and what he persuaded you to do," said Jorden.

In detail, James told him how Boggs had gained influence with the technicians necessary to prepare the plant for destruction, how he had persuaded them that a new, idealistic social order demanded their obedience to this fantastic plan. Then, under the Governor's direction, two of the men betrayed the rest. Only James, who was at a slight distance from his normal operating post that night, had escaped with non-fatal injuries.

"I know how you feel," said James. "You'd like to stick a knife into me now. But until you succeed in disposing of Boggs, you need to be sure I'm alive. When that's over you'll send someone around to take care of the traitor, James. But you may be sure I won't be here. I'll get through your guards!"

The man was half crazed, Jorden thought, from infection and fever in half treated wounds, and probably from the effects of radiation itself. "We aren't going to set up any guards," he said. "We're going to send you medical care. Don't try to get away down the river. I'll have some men who'll take you where you'll be safe and have care."

Jorden left, on the hope that James would not attempt further flight until he was assured of Boggs' defeat. But the colony could not quickly administer the kind of defeat James wanted. They had to be orderly, even if it was a frontier community. There had to be a trial. There had to be evidence, and James had to be called to give it.

He returned to the village and made arrangements with Adamson to get medical care for James. Dr. Babbit, one of the four physicians with the colony, was sufficiently out of sympathy with Boggs to be trusted.

Then, with his family, he accompanied Tibbets to Maintown. On the bulletin board outside the Council Hall he hung an announcement of his candidacy for the governorship, which Tibbets had prepared for him. Tibbets made a little speech to the handful of people who gathered to read what was on the bulletin, but Jorden declined to make any personal statement just now. He had enough to say when it came time to accuse Boggs of the crimes involved in destruction of the power plant.

But among those who squinted closely at Tibbets' fine, black printing there came a look of mild awe. It had been generally assumed that Boggs would go unopposed for re-election.

On the way back Tibbets' car passed the length of Maintown and took them by the deserted house which Jorden had built in their first year on Serrengia. Bonnie gave it a covetous look, contrasting its spaciousness with the primitive cabin in which she now lived.

Tibbets caught her glance. "If it were not for Boggs you would still be living there," he said.

Bonnie made no answer. Both she and Roddy stared ahead, as if unable to bring their attention to bear upon the present, because of the fear incited by everything about them. Jorden was also silent, but his eyes wandered incessantly over the surrounding hills and distant farmlands. He hadn't bargained for anything like this. He had expected to find himself in a society of cooperative and uniformly energetic human beings. He knew now, without any further persuasion, that this had been a vision strictly from an ivory tower.

He should have anticipated that in a group like this there would be a sprinkling of small time thugs and dictators and generally shiftless individuals who could not make a go of it in the society they had left. At home you could live and work with such without ever being more than vaguely aware of their eccentricities. Here, their deviation from required cooperation was enough to disrupt the whole community.

He could understand the terror in Bonnie and Roddy. They had come only because of him, with no understanding of the colony's purpose. The present turmoil underlined their conviction that it had been pure folly to come. Somehow he'd have to show them. He'd have to make them understand there was a reason for being on Serrengia. But at the moment he did not know how to do it.

The program called for a continuation well into the night with a long scene at the cabin, but Ashby interrupted it as soon as they returned from Maintown. He ordered a twenty four hour rest, because of Bonnie. The extended period of sleep wouldn't harm Jorden.

Bonnie, however, was furious at the interruption as she came out of the test pit.

"If you're going to let it go to the end, why don't you get on with it?" she demanded. "The whole thing is so far off the track that you might as well find out as soon as possible that you're not getting anywhere."

"I think we're beginning to find out a great deal. But I want you to have a rest. The hours of this shift are much too long for you."

"You think you know what's going on inside Mark Jorden by watching the dials and meters, but you don't, because it's not himself he's concerned about. It's a goal outside and bigger than himself. The colony means something to him. It never meant anything at all to any of the others."

"Then this is the kind of situation we've been looking for."

"But we haven't the techniques or insight to understand it. We can analyze a man who's running away—but we're not prepared for one who's running toward."

The night after they returned from Maintown a terrific storm broke over the plateau. It began at supper time and for an hour poured torrents of water on the land. Jorden wanted to go down to the river to see if their diversion dams were holding. If they went out it meant long days of hard hand labor restoring them.

He gave in, however, to Bonnie's plea to stay in the house with them. Roddy was frightened of the storm and looked physically ill when thunder made the walls of the cabin shake. It wouldn't change the actual facts of the damage to the dams whether Jorden examined them now or in the morning. He tried to think up stories to tell the children, but it was hard to make up some dealing only with Serrengia and ignoring Earth, as he had to do for Roddy's sake.

After the rain finally stopped and Bonnie had put the children to bed there came a knock at the door. Bonnie opened it. Governor Boggs and two Council members moved into the room. Little pools of water drained to the floor about their feet.

The Governor turned slowly and grinned at Bonnie and Mark Jorden as the light from the lamp and the fireplace fell upon him. "Nasty night out," he said. "For a time I was afraid we weren't going to make it."

Boggs was a short, stout man and carried himself very erect. He seemed to exaggerate his normal posture as he moved toward the chairs Bonnie offered the men.

Jorden remained seated in his big wooden chair by the fireplace glancing up with cold challenge in his face as his visitors settled on the opposite side of the fire.

"I'm sorry we missed you when you were in town today," said Boggs. "It was not until late this afternoon that I became aware of your visit."

He reached to an inner coat pocket and drew forth a paper which he unfolded carefully. Jorden recognized it as the announcement he had tacked on the bulletin board. Boggs passed it over.

"I felt sure you would wish to withdraw this, Jorden, after you had given it a little fuller consideration. I'm sure that by now you have had time to think over the matter a little more calmly and find a good many reasons why you should withdraw your announcement."

"I haven't thought much about it," said Jorden, "but now that you call it to my attention I am becoming aware of an increasing number of reasons why I should not withdraw. I assure you I have no intention of doing so."

Boggs smiled and folded up the paper and slipped it into the fire. "I have not been such a bad administrator during my first term of office, have I Jorden?"

"That is for the people to decide—on election day."

"But why should they want to change a perfectly capable administrator," said Boggs in an injured tone, "and put in a very capable engineer and farm manager—who has no qualifications in administrative matters?"

"That too is a question to be answered on election day."

Boggs shifted in his chair, dropping the deliberately maintained smile from his face. "There have been some stories circulating about the colony recently," he said. "It is possible that you have heard them and believe them."

"Possibly," said Jorden.

"I wouldn't. I wouldn't believe them if I were you. I wouldn't even listen to them because it might lead to dangerous and erroneous conclusions, which would cause you to convict in your mind an honest man."

"That would be my error then, wouldn't it?" said Jorden.

The Governor nodded. "A grave one as far as it concerns the welfare of yourself and your family, Jorden."

Jorden's face hardened. "Threats of that kind aren't appropriate to your position, Governor."

"Perhaps you are not aware of my exact position."

"I think I am! And I intend to do everything in my power to change it. You are a small time chiseler who saw a good chance to set yourself up for life in a cushy situation where five hundred other people would obey your slightest whim. That's an old fashioned situation, Boggs, and you can't set it up here even if you are willing to resort to sabotage and murder."

Boggs eyes narrowed and he looked at Jorden for a long time. "I am afraid, then," he said, "that there is nothing I can do except put a stop to your repeating these lying stories about me."

The Governor's eyes never moved, but Jorden shifted in sudden, wild indecision. Almost simultaneously there were two shots exploding in the narrow cabin, and then a third. Jorden and Boggs leaped out of their chairs.

From the kitchen doorway came the steel-taut voice of Bonnie. "Don't move any further, Mr. Boggs. Put your hands in the air. Get his gun, Mark—in the pocket on this side."

For a moment Jorden hesitated, his eyes held by the sight of Boggs' two gunmen on the floor, blood spreading in tiny rivulets. He took the pistol from the Governor's pocket and held it in readiness.

"I ought to kill you now, Boggs," he said. "Fortunately, or unfortunately, we have to set a precedent in such matters if the colony is to survive. We have to go through the formality of a trial for sabotaging the power plant and murdering those killed there. Actually, it would be a good idea if you just took off over the hills and went as far as you could before the jungle got you. It would save us all a great deal of trouble."

Hope surged in Boggs' eyes as he recognized that Jorden was incapable of shooting him down. Then bitterness mingled with that hope. "You won't get away with this, Jorden. We'll see what the people have to say about your wife shooting my men down while my back is turned."

"Their backs weren't turned," said Jorden. "Get them out of here now. If you want to save explanations as to why you came here tonight you might find a convenient spot and bury them—before you take out over the hills yourself."

Watching until they could no longer see the lights of Boggs' car, they closed the door. Bonnie collapsed with a moan, cringing in Jorden's arms.

"Now they'll kill us all," she said in a lifeless voice. "We haven't got a chance. For this we followed your great dream of colonizing an outpost of the Universe!"

That night Roddy was sick. Six days later he was dead. Before they decided to go through with this section of the program there were long and heated conferences between Bonnie and Ashby and the staff working at the test pit. Bonnie insisted the program should be dropped here. They already knew that Jorden was what they were searching for. They had only to analyze the factors that had brought him to the test and they would have what they needed to identify as many colonists as the project required. He didn't need to be broken down any further.

Ashby knew this was not true. Jorden's basic purpose as a colonist had not yet been brought into sight. Ashby recognized that his goal was almost certainly the perpetuation of the colony—and he was the first one who had maintained such a goal this far—but they had to know the drive that existed behind the goal. If it should develop a basis wholly in flight it would still crack before completion of the program.

But Ashby continued to be hesitant on Bonnie's account. Roddy's illness and death meant a continuous tour in the test pit for the full six days. And this was cut from the scheduled eight it normally occupied. Why it was impossible for Bonnie to reduce her own personal tension on the project, Ashby didn't know, but she had become increasingly susceptible as time went on.

Word of Jorden's persistence was spreading among the staff personnel of other sections of the lab. A subdued excitement was stirring among them. In most cases so far examined, the colonist had by now either knuckled under to Boggs or engaged in a futile personal duel with him. If they went further, they almost invariably collapsed under the pressure of Bonnie's blame and began cursing Serrengia as well as the Earth from which they fled.

Ashby ordered resumption of the program. It was an agony for him, too, watching Bonnie during the long hours of Roddy's illness. It seemed every bit as much a test of her strength and endurance as it was of Mark Jorden's. With the televiewer Ashby brought an image of her face up close, studying her from every angle during the long nights when she and Mark Jorden exchanged vigil over Roddy. He scanned her face by the firelight of the rough cabin.

After three days, Jorden was running close to exhaustion, but in spite of the strain Bonnie seemed capable of remaining there forever. Her eyes watched Jorden's face, taking in his every movement and expression.

And after three days of watching Bonnie's face in close-up, Ashby suddenly murmured aloud to himself in disbelief and astonishment.

Dr. Miller, who was Tibbets in the program, came up to his side. "What is it, Ashby? Has something gone wrong?"

Ashby shook his head slowly in wonder and pointed to the image in the viewer. "Look at her," he said. "Can't you see what has happened to Bonnie? We should have caught it long ago. No wonder this job is tearing her apart—no wonder she doesn't want it to end the way it must—or end at all, for that matter!"

"I still don't see what you are talking about," said Miller in exasperation. "I don't see that anything has happened to her. She looks like the same old Bonnie to me."

"Does she?" said Ashby. "Watch her when she looks at Jorden. Can't you see she has fallen in love with him?"

There was probably a whole class of people like Roddy, Jorden thought. People incapable of surviving beyond the world on which they were born. Since the day of his coming Roddy had fought an unceasing battle with this hated, alien world of Serrengia. He awoke each morning to renew the unequal contest before he was even out of bed—and knowing fully that he was beaten before he started.

Jorden had tried every way he knew to instill into his son some of his own love for this new world. It was a good world and the men who grew up on it in the years to come would love it with all their hearts. But Roddy could not give up his reaching back, his longing for Earth. He shrank before the problem of their doubtful food supply. He caught snatches of adult worries and nourished them with a dark agony that made it appear to Jorden sometimes as if the boy were walking in a nightmare.

It had been cruel and brutal to bring him. But there was no use blaming himself for that. If only Bonnie would stop blaming him! He couldn't have known ahead of time that Roddy was one of those who could not be—transplanted. Fervently, he prayed for the boy's life now and vowed that when the ships came again he would be free to go home.

And always Bonnie's eyes were upon him. Sitting in the firelight of the cabin, he could feel her staring at him, accusing him, hating him for bringing them to Serrengia.

Once he looked up and caught her glance. "Don't hate me so much, Bonnie!" he said. "You're driving Roddy down. I can feel it. Reach out to him with your love and don't let him go."

But Roddy said later that same evening, "Maybe I'll go back to Earth now, Daddy. Do you think that's where little boys go when they die?"

He wanted to return so badly that he was willing to die to achieve it, Jorden thought. That's what Dr. Babbit said: "Roddy doesn't even want to live, Jorden. As incredible as it seems, he's literally dying of homesickness. I'm afraid there's not a thing I can do for him. I'm sorry, but it's up to you. You and Bonnie are the only ones who can give him a desire to remain, if anyone can."

Roddy's hate for Serrengia was greater than any desire they could induce in him to live. With ease, he conquered all the miracle drugs Dr. Babbit lavished from the colony's restricted store. He died on the sixth night after Boggs' visit.

The funeral was held in the little community church built when the colonists first laid out Maintown. Mark and Bonnie Jorden were almost oblivious to the words spoken over the body of Roddy by the Reverend Wagner, who had come as the colonists' spiritual adviser.

Bonnie's hands were folded on her lap, and she kept her eyes down throughout the service. She was aware of the agony within Mark Jorden. It was a real agony, and its strength almost frightened her, for she had never before seen such a response in any man who had gone through the test this far. They were men concerned only with themselves, incapable of the love that Jorden could feel for a son.

He reached out and took one of her hands in his own. She could feel the emotion within him, the tightening and trembling of his big, hard-muscled arm.

Ashby was watching. Over the private communication system that linked them he murmured, "Cry, Bonnie! Make it real. Make him hate himself and everything he's done since he decided to become a colonist—if you can! This is where we've got to find out whether he can crack or not—and why."

"You can't break him," said Bonnie. "He's the strongest man I've ever known. If you find his breaking point it will be when you destroy him utterly. You've got to quit before you reach that point!"

"All that we've done will be useless if we quit now, Bonnie. Just a few more hours and then it will all be over—"

As if his words had touched a hidden trigger, she did begin to cry with a deep but almost inaudible sound and a heavy movement of her shoulders. Mark Jorden put his arm about her as if to force away her grief.

"I know, Bonnie," said Ashby softly. "I can see in your face what's happened to you. It's going to be all right. Everything doesn't end for you when the test is over."

"Oh, shut up!" said Bonnie in a sudden rage that made her tears come faster. "If I ever work on another of your damned experiments it will be when I've lost my senses entirely! You don't know what this does to people. I didn't know either—because I didn't care. But now I know—"

"You know that no harm results after we've erased and corrected all inadequate reactions at the end of the test. You're letting your feelings cover up your full awareness of what we're doing."

"Yes, and I suppose that when it's over I had better submit to a little erasing myself. Then Bonnie can go back to work as a little iced steel probe for some more of your guinea pigs!"

"Bonnie—!"

She made no answer to Ashby, but lay her head on Jorden's shoulder while her sobbing subsided. How did it happen? she asked herself. It wasn't anything she had wanted. It had just happened. It had happened that first day when he came in from the field at the beginning of the experiment with all of the planted background that made him think he was meeting Bonnie for the thousandth time instead of the first.

She was supposed to be an actress and receive his husbandly kiss with all the skilled mimicry that made her so valuable to the lab. But it hadn't been like that. She had played sister, mother, daughter, wife—a hundred roles to as many other tested applicants. For the first time she saw one as a human being instead of a sociological specimen. That's the way it was when she met Mark Jorden.

There was no answer to it, she thought bitterly as she rested her face against his shoulder. Ashby was right—just a few more hours and it would all be over. All Jorden's feeling for her as his wife was induced by the postulates of the test, just as were his feelings for Roddy. His subjective reactions were real enough, but they would vanish when their stimulus was removed with the test postulates. He would look upon the restored Roddy as just another little boy—and upon Bonnie, the Doctor in Sociology, as just another misemployed female.

She raised her head and dried her eyes as she sensed that the service was ending. Actually, Ashby was right, of course. They had to go on, and the sooner it came to an end the better it would be for her. She would submit to alteration of her own personal data after the test, she thought. She would let them erase all feelings and sentiments she held for Mark Jorden, and then she would be as good as new. After all, if a sociologist couldn't handle his own reactions in a situation of this kind he wasn't of much value in his profession!

The sun was hot as they returned from the little burial ground near the church. There were quite a number of other graves besides Roddy's, but his was the loneliest, Jorden thought. He had never forgiven them for robbing him of his home and the only world in which he could live.

He felt the growing coldness of Bonnie as they came up to their shabby cabin that had once looked so brave to him. Serrengia had cost him Bonnie, too. Even before Roddy. She had remained only because it was her duty.

He took her hand as she put a foot on the doorstep. "Bonnie—"

She looked at him bitterly, her eyes searching his face as if to find something of the quality that once drew her to him. "Don't try to say it, Mark—there's nothing left to say."

He let her go, and the two children followed past him into the house. He sat down on the step and looked out over the fields that edged the river bank. His mind felt numbed by Roddy's passing. Bonnie's insistent blame made him live it over and over again.

The light from the green of the fields was like a caress to his eyes. I should hate it, he thought. I should hate the whole damned planet for what it's taken from me. But that's not right— Serrengia hasn't taken anything. It's only that Bonnie and I can't live in the same world, or live the same kind of lives. Roddy was like her. But I didn't know then. I didn't know how either of them were.

We have to go on. There's no going back. Maybe if I'd known, I would have made it different for all of us. I can't now, and it would be crazy to start hating Serrengia for the faults that are in us. Who could do anything but love this fresh, wild planet of ours—?

He ought to go down and take a look at the field, he thought. He rose to go in and tell Bonnie. The crops hadn't had water since Roddy took sick.

He found Bonnie in the bedroom with the drawers of their cabinets open and their trunk in the middle of the floor, its lid thrown back. Clothes lay strewn on the bed.

He felt a slow tightening of his scalp and of the skin along the back of his neck. "Bonnie—"

She straightened and looked into his face with cold, distant eyes. "I'm packing, Mark," she said. "I'm leaving. I'm going home. The girls are going with me. You can stay until they dig your grave beside Roddy's, but I'm going home."

Jorden's face went white. He strode forward and caught her by the arms. "Bonnie—you know there's no way to go home. There won't be a ship for six years. This is home, Bonnie. There's no other place to go."

For a moment the set expression of her face seemed to melt. She frowned as if he had told her some mystery she could not fathom. Then her countenance cleared and its blank determination returned. "I'm going home," she repeated. "You can't stop me. I've done all a wife can be expected to do. I've given my son as the price of your foolishness. You can't ask for more."

He had to get out. He felt that if he remained another instant just then something inside him would explode under the pressure of his grief. He went to the front door and stood leaning against it while he looked over the landscape that almost seemed to reach out for him in hate as it had for Roddy. So you want her, too! he cried inside himself.

Alice came up and tugged at his hand as he stood there. "What's the matter, Daddy? What's the matter with Mama?"

He bent down and kissed her on the forehead. "Nothing, honey. You go and play for a moment while I help Mother."

"I want to help, too!"

"Please, Alice—"

He moved back to the bedroom. Bonnie was carefully examining each item of apparel she packed in the big trunk. She didn't look up as he came in.

"Bonnie," he said in a low voice, "are you going to leave me?"

She put down the dress she was holding and looked up at him. "Yes I'm leaving you," she said. "You've got what you wanted— all you've ever wanted." She looked out towards the fields, shimmering in the heat of the day.

"That's not true, Bonnie. You know it isn't. I've always loved you and needed you, and it's grown greater every hour we've been together."

"Then you'll have to prove it! Give up this hell-world you want us to call home, and give us back our Earth. If you love me, you can prove it."

"It's no test of love to make a man give up the goal that means his life to him. You'd despise me forever if I let you do that to me. I'd rather you went away from me now with the feeling you have at this time, because I'd know I had your love—"

Bonnie remained still and unmoving in his arms, her face averted from his. He put his hand to her chin and turned her face to him. "You do love me, Bonnie? That hasn't changed, has it?"

She put her head against his chest and rocked from side to side as if in some agony. "Oh, no—Mark! That will never change. Damn you, Ashby, damn you—"

In the control room Ashby and Miller groaned aloud to each other, and a technician looked at them questioningly, his hand on a switch. Ashby shook his head and stared at the scene before him.

Jorden shook Bonnie gently in his arms. "Ashby?" he said. "Who's Ashby?"

Bonnie looked up, the blank despair on her face again. "I don't remember—" she said haltingly. "Someone I used to—know—"

"It makes no difference," Jorden said. "What matters is that you love me and you're going to stay with me. Let's put these things away now, darling. I know how you've felt the past week, but we've got to put it behind us and look forward to the future. Roddy would want it that way."

"There's no future to look forward to," said Bonnie dully. "Nothing here on Serrengia. There's no meaning to any of us being here. I'm going back to Earth."

"It does have a meaning! If I could only make you see it. If you could only understand why I had to come—"

"Then tell me if you know! You've never tried to tell me. You live as if you know something so deep and secret you can live by it every hour of your life and find meaning in it. But I can only guess at what it is you've chosen for your god. If it's anything but some illusion, put it into words and make me know it, too!"

"I've never tried," said Jorden hesitantly. "I've never tried to put it into words. It's something I didn't know was in me until I heard of the chance to colonize Serrengia. And then I knew I had to come.

"It's like a growing that you feel in every cell. It's a growing out and away, and it's what you have to do. You're a sperm—an ovum—and if you don't leave the parent body you die. You don't have to hate what you leave behind as James and Boggs and so many of the others do. It gave you life, and for that you're grateful. But you've got to have a life of your own.

"It's what I was born to do, Bonnie. I didn't know it was there, but now I've found it I can't kill it."

"You have to kill it—or me."

"You don't mean that. You're part of me. You've been a part of me so long you feel what I feel. You're lying, Bonnie, when you say you're going away. You don't want to go. You want to go on with me, but something's holding you back. What is it, Bonnie? Tell me what it is that holds you back!"

Her eyes went wide. For a moment she thought he was talking

out of the real situation, not the make-believe of the test. Then she recognized the impossibility of this. Her eyes cast a pleading glance in the direction of the observation tubes.

Ashby spoke fiercely: "Go on, Bonnie! Don't lose the tension. Push him. We've got to know. He's almost there!"

She moved slowly to the dresser where she had laid Jorden's hunting knife previously, as if with no particular intent. Now, out of sight of Jorden, her hand touched it. She picked it up.

Ashby's voice came again. "Bonnie—move!"

She murmured, "Lost—"

And then she whirled about, knife in hand. She cried aloud. "I can't go on any further! Can't you see this is enough? Stop it! Stop it—"

Jorden leaped for the knife.

In the observation room a technician touched a switch.

Ashby felt the subdued elation of success reached after a long and strenuous effort. Bonnie was seated across the desk from him, but he sat at an angle so that he could see the four hulls out of the corner of his eye. One and Two had made their test flights and the others would not be far behind. The expedition would be a success, too. There was no longer any doubt of that, because he knew now where to look for adequate personnel.

"I'm glad I didn't foul up your test completely, anyway," said Bonnie slowly. "Even if what you say about Mark shouldn't turn out to be true."

Ashby moved his chair around to face her directly. She was rested, and had gone through a mental re-orientation which had removed some of the tension from her face.

"You didn't foul it up at all," he said. "We went far enough to learn that he would have survived even your suicide, and would have continued in his determination to carry the colony forward. Nothing but his own death will stand in his way if he actually sets out on such a project. Are you completely sure you want to be tied to such a single purposed man as Mark Jorden is?"

"There's no doubt of that! But I just don't feel as if I can face him now—with his knowing.... How can I ever be sure his feeling for me was not merely induced by the test experience, and might change as time goes on? You should have wiped it all out, and let us start over from scratch. It would have been easier that way."

"There isn't time enough before the ships leave. But why should we have erased it all? We took away the postulates of the test and left Bonnie in his memory. His love for you didn't vanish when the test postulates went. As long as he has a memory of you he will love you. So why make him fall in love with you twice? No use wasting so much important time at your age. Here he comes—"

Bonnie felt she couldn't possibly turn around as the door opened behind her. She heard Mark's moment of hesitation, his slow steps on the carpet. Ashby was smiling a little and nodding. Then she felt the hard grip of Mark's hands on her shoulders. He drew her up and turned her to face him. Her eyes were wet.

"Bonnie—" he said softly.

Ashby turned to the window again. The gantry cranes were hoisting machinery in Hull Three. Maybe he had been wrong about there not being enough time between now and takeoff for Mark and Bonnie to discover each other all over again. They worked pretty fast. But then, as he had mentioned, why waste time at their age?

They were smiling, holding tight to each other as Ashby turned back from the window.

"They tell me I passed," said Jorden. "I'm sorry about taking your best Social Examiner away from you—but as you told me in the beginning this colonization business is a family affair."

"Yes—that happens to be one of the few things I was right about." Ashby motioned them to the chairs. "Through you we located our major error. It was our identifying rebellion with colonization ability. Colonization is not a matter of rebellion at all. The two factors merely happen to accompany each other at times. But the essence of colonization is a growth factor—of the kind you so very accurately described when Bonnie pushed you into digging up some insight on the matter. It is so often associated with rebellion because rebellion is or has been, historically, necessary to the exercise of this growth factor.

"The American Colonists, for example, were rebels only incidentally. As a group, they possessed a growth factor forcing them beyond the confines of the culture in which they lived. It gave them the strength for rebellion and successful colonization. And it is so easy to confuse colonists of that type with mere cutthroats, thugs, and misfits. The latter may or may not have a sufficiently high growth factor. In any case, their primary drive is hate and fear, which are wholly inadequate motives for successful colonization.

"The ideal colonist does not break with the parent body, nor does he merely extend it. He creates a new nucleus capable of interchange with the parent body, but not controlled by it. He wants to build beyond the current society, and the latter is not strong enough to pull him back into it. Colonization may take everything else of value in life and give nothing but itself in return, but the colonists' desire for new life and growth is great enough to make this sufficient. It is not a mere transplant of an old life. It is conception and gestation and birth.

"Our present society allows almost unlimited exercise of the growth factor in individuals, regardless of how powerful it may be. That is why we have failed to colonize the planets. They offer no motive or satisfaction sufficient to outweigh the satisfactions already available. As a result we've had virtually no applicants coming to us because of hampered growth. You are one of the very few who might come under our present approach. And even a very slight change of occupational conditions would have kept you from coming. You didn't want the department leadership offered you, because it would limit the personally creative functions you enjoyed. That one slim, hairbreadth factor brought you in."

"But how do you expect now to get any substantial number of colonists?" exclaimed Jorden.

"We'll put on a recruiting campaign. We'll go to the creative groups—the engineers, the planners, the artists—we'll show that opportunity for creative functioning and growth will be far greater in the work of building colonial outposts than in any activity they now enjoy. And we won't have to exaggerate, either. It's true.

"We'll be able to send out a colony of whom we can be certain. In the past, colonies have invariably failed when they consisted only of members fleeing from something, without possessing an adequate growth factor.

"When this becomes thoroughly understood in my field, I shall probably never live down my initial error of assuming that a colonist had to hate or fear what he left behind in order to leave it forever. The exact opposite is true. Successful colonization of the Universe by Earthmen will occur only when there is a love and respect for the Homeland—and a capacity for complete independence from it."

Ashby pressed his fingers together and looked at his visitors soberly. "There is only one thing further," he said. "We've found out also that Bonnie is not essentially a colonist—"

Bonnie's face went white. She pushed Jorden's arm away and leaned across the desk. "You knew—! Then we can't—Why didn't you tell me this in the beginning?"

"Please don't be hasty, Bonnie," said Ashby. "As I was about to say, we have found, however, that another condition exists in which you can become eligible and stable through a genuine love for a qualified colonist, to the extent you are willing to follow him completely in his ambitions and desires. This is strictly a feminine possibility—a woman can become a sort of second order colonist, you might say.

"Of course, Jorden, you still have to make the basic decision as to whether you want to go to Serrengia or not. We have found out merely that you can."

"I think there's no doubt about my wanting to," said Jorden.

He turned Bonnie around in his arms again, and Ashby chuckled mildly. "I have always said there is no piece of data you cannot find, provided you can devise the proper experimental procedure for turning it up," he said.

THE UNLEARNED

The Chief Officer of Scientific Services, Information and Coordination was a somewhat misleading and obscure title, and Dr. Sherman Hockley who held it was not the least of those whom the title misled and sometimes obscured.

He told himself he was not a mere library administrator, although he was proud of the information files built up under his direction. They contained the essence of accumulated knowledge found to date on Earth and the extraterrestrial planets so far contacted. He didn't feel justified in claiming to be strictly a research supervisor, either, in spite of duties as top level administrator for all divisions of the National Standardization and Research Laboratories and their subsidiaries in government, industry, and education. During his term of supervision the National Laboratories had made a tremendous growth, in contrast to a previous decline.

Most of all, however, he disclaimed being a figurehead, to which all the loose strings of a vast and rambling organization could be tied. But sometimes it was quite difficult to know whether or not that was his primary assignment after all. His unrelenting efforts to keep out of the category seemed to be encountering more and more determination to push him in that direction.

Of course, this was merely the way it looked in his more bitter moments—such as the present. Normally, he had a full awareness of the paramount importance of his position, and was determined to administer it on a scale in keeping with that importance. His decision could affect the research in the world's major laboratories. Not that he was a dictator by any means, although there were times when dictation was called for. As when a dozen projects needed money and the Congress allotted enough for one or two. Somebody had to make a choice—

His major difficulty was that active researchers knew it was the Congressional Science Committee which was ultimately responsible for their bread and butter. And the Senators regarded the scientists, who did the actual work in the laboratories, as the only ones who mattered. Both groups tended to look upon Hockley's office as a sort of fulcrum in their efforts to maintain balance with each other—or as referee in their sparring for adequate control over each other.

At that, however, things research-wise were better than ever before. More funds and facilities were available. Positions in pure research were more secure.

And then, once again, rumors about Rykeman III had begun to circulate wildly a few days ago.

Since Man's achievement of extra-galactic flight, stories of Rykeman III had tantalized the world and made research scientists sick with longing when they considered the possible truth of what they heard. The planet was rumored to be a world of super-science, whose people had an answer for every research problem a man could conceive. The very few Earthmen who had been to Rykeman III confirmed the rumors. It was a paradise, according to their stories. And among other peoples of the galaxies the inhabitants of Rykeman III were acknowledged supreme in scientific achievement. None challenged them. None even approached them in abilities.

What made the situation so frustrating to Earthmen was the additional report that the Rykes were quite altruistically sharing their science with a considerable number of other worlds on a fee basis. Earth scientists became intoxicated at the mere thought of studying at the feet of the exalted Rykes.

Except Dr. Sherman Hockley. From the first he had taken a dim view of the Ryke reports. Considering the accomplishments of the National Laboratories, he could see no reason for his colleagues' half-shameful disowning of all their own work in favor of a completely unknown culture several hundred million light years away. They were bound to contact more advanced cultures in their explorations—and could be thankful they were as altruistic as the Rykes!—but it was no reason to view themselves as idiot children hoping to be taught by the Rykes.

He had kept his opinions very much to himself in the past, since they were not popular with his associates, who generally regarded his attitudes as simply old-fashioned. But now, for the first time, a Ryke ship was honoring Earth with a visit. There was almost hysterical speculation over the possibility that Earth would be offered tutelage by the mighty Ryke scientists. Hockley wouldn't have said he was unalterably opposed to the idea. He would have described himself as extremely cautious. What he did oppose wholeheartedly was the enthusiasm that painted the Rykes with pure and shining light, without a shadowy hue in the whole picture.

Since his arrival, the Ryke envoy had been closeted with members of the Congressional Science Committee. Not a word had leaked as to his message. Shortly, however, the scientists were to be let in on the secret which might affect their careers for better or for worse during the rest of their lives, and for many generations to come. The meeting was going to be—

Hockley jumped to his feet as he glanced at the clock. He hurried through the door to the office of his secretary, Miss Cardston, who looked meaningfully at him as he passed.

"I'll bet there isn't a Senator on time," he said.

In the corridor he almost collided with Dr. Lester Showalter, who was his Administrative Assistant for Basic Research. "The Ryke character showed up fifteen minutes ago," said Showalter. "Everyone's waiting."

"We've got six minutes yet," said Hockley. He walked rapidly beside Showalter. "Is there any word on what the envoy's got that's so important?"

"No. I've got the feeling it's something pretty big. Wheeler and Johnson of Budget are there. Somebody said it might have something to do with the National Lab."

"I don't see the connection between that and a meeting with the Ryke," said Hockley.

Showalter stopped at the door of the conference room. "Maybe they want to sell us something. At any rate, we're about to find out."

The conference table was surrounded by Senators of the

Committee. Layered behind them were scientists representing the cream of Hockley's organization. Senator Markham, the bulky, red-faced Chairman greeted them. "Your seats are reserved at the head of the table," he said.

"Sorry about the time," Hockley mumbled. "Clock must be slow."

"Quite all right. We assembled just a trifle early. I want you to meet our visitor, Special Envoy from Rykeman III, Liacan."

Markham introduced them, and the stick-thin envoy arose with an extended hand. His frail, whistling voice that was in keeping with his bird-like character spoke in clear tones. "I am happy to know you, Dr. Hockley, Dr. Showalter."

The two men sat down in good view of the visitor's profile. Hockley had seen the Rykes before, but had always been repelled by their snobbish approach. Characteristically, the envoy bore roughly anthropomorphic features, including a short feather covering on his dorsal side. He was dressed in bright clothing that left visible the streak of feathering that descended from the bright, plumed crown and along the back of his neck. Gravity and air pressure of Earth were about normal for him. For breathing, however, he was required to wear a small device in one narrow nostril. This was connected to a compact tank on his shoulder.

Markham called for order and introduced the visitor. There was a round of applause. Liacan bowed with a short, stiff gesture and let his small black eyes dart over the audience. With an adjustment of his breathing piece he began speaking.

"It is recognized on Earth," he said, "as it is elsewhere, that my people of Rykeman III possess undisputed intellectual leadership in the galaxies of the Council. Your research is concerned with things taught only in the kindergartens of my world. Much that you hold to be true is in error, and your most profound discoveries are self-evident to the children of my people."

Hockley felt a quick, painful contraction in the region of his diaphragm. So this was it!

"We are regarded with much jealousy, envy, and even hatred by some of our unlearned neighbors in space," said the Ryke. "But it has never been our desire to be selfish with our superior achievements which make us the object of these feelings. We have undertaken a program of scientific leadership in our interstellar neighborhood. This began long before you came into space and many worlds have accepted the plan we offer.

"Obviously, it is impractical to pour out all the knowledge and basic science we have accumulated. Another world would find it impossible to sort out that which was applicable to it. What we do is act as a consultation center upon which others can call at will to obtain data pertaining to any problem at hand. Thus, they are not required to sort through wholly inapplicable information to find what they need.

"For example, if you desire to improve your surface conveyances, we will supply you with data for building an optimum vehicle suitable for conditions on Earth and which is virtually indestructible. You will of course do your own manufacturing, but even there we can supply you with technology that will make the process seem miraculous by your present standards.

"Our services are offered for a fee, payable in suitable items of goods or raw materials. When you contemplate the freedom from monotonous and unending research in fields already explored by us, I am certain you will not consider our fees exorbitant. Our desire is to raise the cultural level of all peoples to the maximum of which they are capable. We know it is not possible or even desirable to bring others to our own high levels, but we do offer assistance to all cultures in accord with their ability to receive. The basic principle is that they shall ask—and whatever is asked for, with intelligence sufficient for its utilization, that shall be granted.

"I am certain I may count on your acceptance of the generous offer of my people."

The envoy sat down with a jiggling of his bright plume, and there was absolute silence in the room. Hockley pictured to himself the dusty, cobweb laboratories of Earth vacated by scientists who ran to the phone to call the Rykes for answers to every problem.

Senator Markham stood up and glanced over the audience. "There is the essence of the program which has been submitted to us," he said. "There is a vast amount of detail which is, of course, obvious to the minds of our friends on Rykeman III, but which must be the subject of much deliberation on the part of us comparatively simple minded Earthmen." He gave a self-conscious chuckle, which got no response.

Hockley felt mentally stunned. Here at last was the thing that had been hoped for by most, anxiously awaited by a few, and opposed by almost no one.

"The major difficulty," said Markham with slow dignity, "is the price. It's high, yes. In monetary terms, approximately twelve and a half billions per year. But certainly no man in his right mind would consider any reasonable figure too high for what we can expect to receive from our friends of Rykeman III.

"We of the Science Committee do not believe, however, that we could get a commitment for this sum to be added to our normal budget. Yet there is a rather obvious solution. The sum required is very close to that which is now expended on the National Standardization and Research Laboratories."

Hockley felt a sudden chill at the back of his neck.

"With the assistance of the Rykes," said Markham, "we shall have no further need of the National Laboratories. We shall require but a small staff to analyze our problems and present them to the Rykes and relay the answers for proper assimilation. Acceptance of the Ryke program provides its own automatic financing!"

He glanced about with a triumphant smile. Hockley felt as if he were looking through a mist upon something that happened a long time ago. The National Lab! Abandon the National Lab!

Around him there were small nods of agreement from his colleagues. Some pursed their lips as if doubtful—but not very much. He waited for someone to rise to his feet in a blast of protest. No one did. For a moment Hockley's own hands tensed on the back of the chair in front of him. Then he slumped back to his seat. Now was not the time.

They had to thrash it out among themselves. He had to show them the magnitude of this bribe. He had to find an argument to beat down the Congressmen's irrational hopes of paradise. He couldn't plead for the Lab on the grounds of sentiment—or that it was sometimes a good idea to work out your own problems. The Senators didn't care for the problems or concerns of the scientists. It appeared that even the scientists themselves had forgotten to care. He had to slug both groups with something very solid.

Markham was going on. "We are convinced this is a bargain which even the most obstinate of our Congressional colleagues will be quick to recognize. It would be folly to compute with building blocks when we can gain access to giant calculators. There should be no real difficulty in getting funds transferred from the National Laboratory.

"At this time we will adjourn. Liacan leaves this evening. Our acceptance of this generous offer will be conveyed to Rykeman III directly upon official sanction by the Congress. I wish to ask this same group to meet again for discussion of the details incident to this transfer of operations. Let us say at ten o'clock in the morning, gentlemen."

Hockley said goodbye to the envoy. Afterwards, he moved through the circle of Senators to his own group. In the corridor they tightened about him and followed along as if he had given an order for them to follow him. He turned and attempted a grin.

71

"Looks like a bull session is in order, gents. Assembly in five minutes in my office."

As he and Showalter opened the door to Miss Cardston's office and strode in, the secretary looked up with a start. "I thought you were going to meet in the conference room."

"We've met," said Hockley. "This is the aftermeeting. Send out for a couple of cases of beer." He glanced at the number surging through the doorway and fished in his billfold. "Better make it three. This ought to cover it."

With disapproval, Miss Cardston picked up the bills and turned to the phone. Almost simultaneously there was a bellow of protest and an enormous, ham-like hand gripped her slender wrist. She glanced up in momentary fright.

Dr. Forman K. Silvers was holding her wrist with one hand and clapping Hockley on the back with the other. "This is not an occasion for beer, my boy!" he said in an enormous voice. "Make that a case of champagne, Miss Cardston." He released her and drew out his own billfold.

"Get somebody to bring in a couple of dozen chairs," Hockley said.

In his own office he walked to the window behind his desk and stood facing it. The afternoon haze was coming up out of the ocean. Faintly visible were the great buildings of the National Laboratories on the other side of the city. Above the mist the sun caught the tip of the eight story tower where the massive field tunnels of the newly designed gammatron were to be installed.

Or were to have been installed.

The gammatron was expected to make possible the creation of gravitational fields up to five thousand g's. It would probably be a mere toy to the Rykes, but Hockley felt a fierce pride in its creation. Maybe that was childish. Maybe his whole feeling about the Lab was childish. Perhaps the time had come to give up childish things and take upon themselves adulthood.

But looking across the city at the concrete spire of the gammatron, he didn't believe it.

He heard the clank of metal chairs as a couple of clerks began bringing them in. Then there was the clink of glassware. He turned to see Miss Cardston stiffly indicating a spot on the library table for the glasses and the frosty bottles.

Hockley walked slowly to the table and filled one of the glasses. He raised it slowly. "It's been a short life but a merry one, gentlemen." He swallowed the contents of the glass too quickly and returned to his desk.

"You don't sound very happy about the whole thing," said Mortenson, a chemist who wore a neat, silvery mustache.

"Are you overjoyed," said Hockley, "that we are to swap the National Lab for a bottomless encyclopedia?"

"Yes, I think so," said Mortenson. "There are some minor objections, but in the end I'm certain we'll all be satisfied with what we get."

"Satisfied! Happy!" exclaimed the mathematician, Dr. Silvers.

"How can you use words so prosaic and restrained in references to these great events which we shall be privileged to witness in our lifetimes?"

He had taken his stand by the library table and was now filling the glasses with the clear, bubbling champagne, sloshing it with ecstatic abandon over the table and the rug.

Hockley glanced toward him. "You don't believe, then, Dr. Silvers, that we should maintain any reserve in regard to the Rykes?"

"None whatever! The gods themselves have stepped down and offered an invitation direct to paradise. Should we question or hold back, or say we are merely happy. The proper response of a man about to enter heaven is beyond words!"

The bombast of the mathematician never failed to enliven any backroom session in which he participated. "I have no doubt," he said, "that within a fortnight we shall be in possession of a solution to the Legrandian Equations. I have sought this for forty years."

"I think it would be a mistake to support the closing of the National Laboratories," said Hockley slowly.

As if a switch had been thrown, their expressions changed. There was a sudden carefulness in their stance and movements, as if they were feinting before a deadly opponent.

"I don't feel it's such a bad bargain," said a thin, bespectacled physicist named Judson. He was seated across the room from Hockley. "I'll vote to sacrifice the Lab in exchange for what the Rykes will give us."

"That's the point," said Hockley. "Exactly what are the Rykes going to give us? And we speak very glibly of sharing their science. But shall we actually be in any position to share it? What becomes of the class of scientists on Earth when the Lab is abandoned?"

Wilkins stood abruptly, his hands shoved part way into his pockets and his lower jaw extended tensely. "I don't believe that's part of this question," he said. "It is not just we scientists who are to share the benefits of the Rykes. It is Mankind. At this time we have no right to consider mere personal concerns. We would betray our whole calling—our very humanity—if we thought for one moment of standing in the way of this development because of our personal concern over economic and professional problems. There has never been a time when a true scientist would not put aside his personal concerns for the good of all."

Hockley waited, half expecting somebody to start clapping. No one did, but there were glances of self-righteous approval in Wilkins' direction. The biologist straightened the sleeves of his coat with a smug gesture and awaited Hockley's rebuttal.

"We are Mankind," Hockley said finally. "You and I are as much a part of humanity as that bus load of punch machine clerks and store managers passing on the street outside. If we betray ourselves we have betrayed humanity.

"This is not a sudden thing. It is the end point of a trend which has gone on for a long time. It began with our first contacts beyond the galaxy, when we realized there were peoples far in advance of us in science and economy. We have been feeding on them ever since. Our own developments have shrunk in direct proportion. For a long time we've been on the verge of becoming intellectual parasites in the Universe. Acceptance of the Ryke offer will be the final step in that direction."

Instantly, almost every other man in the room was talking at once. Hockley smiled faintly until the angry voices subsided. Then Silvers cleared his throat gently. He placed his glass beside the bottles on the table with a precise motion. "I am sure," he said, "that a moment's thought will convince you that you do not mean what you have just said.

"Consider the position of pupil and teacher. One of Man's greatest failings is his predilection for assuming always the position of teacher and eschewing that of pupil. There is also the question of humility, intellectual humility. We scientists have always boasted of our readiness to set aside one so-called truth and accept another with more valid supporting evidence.

"Since our first contact with other galactic civilizations we have had the utmost need to adopt an attitude of humility. We have been fortunate in coming to a community of worlds where war and oppression are not standard rules of procedure. Among our own people we have encountered no such magnanimity as has been extended repeatedly by other worlds, climaxed now by the Ryke's magnificent offer.

"To adopt sincere intellectual humility and the attitude of the pupil is not to function as a parasite, Dr. Hockley."

"Your analogy of teacher and pupil is very faulty in expressing our relation to the Rykes," said Hockley. "Or perhaps I should say it is too hellishly accurate. Would you have us remain the eternal pupils? The closing of the National Laboratories means an irreversible change in our position. Is it worth gaining a universe of knowledge to give up your own personal free inquiry?"

"I am sure none of us considers he is giving up his personal free inquiry," said Silvers almost angrily. "We see unlimited expansion beyond anything we have imagined in our wildest dreams."

On a few faces there were frowns of uncertainty, but no one spoke up to support him. Hockley knew that until this vision of paradise wore off there were none of them on whom he could count.

He smiled broadly and stood up to ease the tension in the room. "Well, it appears you have made your decision. Of course, Congress can accept the Ryke plan whether we approve or not, but it is good to go on record one way or the other. I suppose that on the way out tonight it would be proper to check in at Personnel and file a services available notification."

And then he wished he hadn't said that. Their faces grew a little more set at his unappreciated attempt at humor.

Showalter remained after the others left. He sat across the desk while Hockley turned back to the window. Only the tip of the gammatron tower now caught the late afternoon sunlight.

"Maybe I'm getting old," Hockley said. "Maybe they're right and the Lab isn't worth preserving if it means the difference between getting or not getting tutelage from the Rykes."

"But you don't feel that's true," said Showalter.

"No."

"You're the one who built the Lab into what it is. It has as much worth as it ever had, and you have an obligation to keep it from being destroyed by a group of politicians who could never understand its necessity."

"I didn't build it," said Hockley. "It grew because I was able to find enough people who wanted the institution to exist. But I've been away from research so long—I never was much good at it really. Did you ever know that? I've always thought of myself as a sort of impressario of scientific productions, if I might use such a term. Maybe those closer to the actual work are right. Maybe I'm just trying to hang on to the past. It could be time for a jump to a new kind of progress."

"You don't believe any of that."

Hockley looked steadily in the direction of the Lab buildings. "I don't believe any of it. That isn't just an accumulation of buildings over there, with a name attached to them. It's the advancing terminal of all Man's history of trying to find out about himself and the Universe. It started before Neanderthal climbed into his caves a half million years ago. From then until now there's a steady path of trial and error—of learning. There's exultation and despair, success and failure. Now they want to say it was all for nothing."

"But to be pupils—to let the Rykes teach us—"

"The only trouble with Silvers' argument is that our culture has

78

never understood that teaching, in the accepted sense, is an impossibility. There can be only learning—never teaching. The teacher has to be eliminated from the actual learning process before genuine learning can ever take place. But the Rykes offer to become the Ultimate Teacher."

"And if this is true," said Showalter slowly, "you couldn't teach it to those who disagree, could you? They'd have to learn it for themselves."

Hockley turned. For a moment he continued to stare at his assistant. Then his face broke into a narrow grin. "Of course you're right! There's only one way they'll ever learn it: go through the actual experience of what Ryke tutelage will mean."

Most of the workrooms at Information Central were empty this time of evening. Hockley selected the first one he came to and called for every scrap of data pertaining to Rykeman III. There was a fair amount of information available on the physical characteristics of the world. Hockley scribbled swift, privately intelligible notes as he scanned. The Rykes lived under a gravity one third heavier than Earth's, with a day little more than half as long, and they received only forty percent as much heat from their frail sun as Earthmen were accustomed to.

Cultural characteristics included a trading system that made the entire planet a single economic unit. And the planet had no history whatever of war. The Rykes themselves had contributed almost nothing to the central libraries of the galaxies concerning their own personal makeup and mental functions, however. What little was available came from observers not of their race.

There were indications they were a highly unemotional race, not given to any artistic expression. Hockley found this surprising. The general rule was for highly intellectual attainments to be accompanied by equally high artistic expression.

But all of this provided no data that he could relate to his present problem, no basis for argument beyond what he already had. He returned the films to their silver cans and sat staring at the neat pile of them on the desk. Then he smiled at his own obtuseness. Data on Rykeman III might be lacking, but the Ryke plan had been tried on plenty of other worlds. Data on them should not be so scarce.

He returned the cans and punched out a new request on the call panel. Twenty seconds later he was pleasantly surprised by a score of new tapes in the hopper. That was enough for a full night's work. He wished he'd brought Showalter along to help.

Then his eye caught sight of the label on the topmost can in the pile: Janisson VIII. The name rang a familiar signal somewhere deep in his mind. Then he knew—that was the home world of Waldon Thar, one of his closest friends in the year when he'd gone to school at Galactic Center for advanced study.

Thar had been one of the most brilliant researchers Hockley had ever known. In bull session debate he was instantly beyond the depth of everyone else.

Janisson VIII. Thar could tell him about the Rykes!

Hockley pushed the tape cans aside and went to the phone in the workroom. He dialed for the interstellar operator. "Government priority call to Janisson VIII," he said. "Waldon Thar. He attended Galactic Center Research Institute twenty-three years ago. He came from the city Plar, which was his home at that time. I have no other information, except that he is probably employed as a research scientist."

There was a moment's silence while the operator noted the information. "There will be some delay," she said finally. "At present the inter-galactic beams are full."

"I can use top emergency priority on this," said Hockley. "Can you clear a trunk for me on that?"

"Yes. One moment, please."

He sat by the window for half an hour, turning down the light in the workroom so that he could see the flow of traffic at the port west of the Lab buildings. Two spaceships took off and three came in while he waited. And then the phone rang.

"I'm sorry," the operator said. "Waldon Thar is reported not on Janisson VIII. He went to Rykeman III about two Earth years ago. Do you wish to attempt to locate him there?"

"By all means," said Hockley. "Same priority."

This was better than he had hoped for. Thar could really get him the information he needed on the Rykes. Twenty minutes later the phone rang again. In the operator's first words Hockley sensed apology and knew the attempt had failed.

"Our office has learned that Waldon Thar is at present on tour as aide to the Ryke emissary, Liacan. We can perhaps trace—"

"No!" Hockley shouted. "That won't be necessary. I know now—"

81

He almost laughed aloud to himself. This was an incredible piece of good luck. Waldon Thar was probably out at the space port right now—unless one of those ships taking off had been the Ryke—

He wondered why Thar had not tried to contact him. Of course, it had been a long time, but they had been very close at the center. He dialed the field control tower. "I want to know if the ship from Rykeman III has departed yet," he said.

"They were scheduled for six hours ago, but mechanical difficulty has delayed them. Present estimated take-off is 1100."

Almost two hours to go, Hockley thought. That should be time enough. "Please put me in communication with one of the aides aboard named Waldon Thar. This is Sherman Hockley of Scientific Services. Priority request."

"I'll try, sir." The tower operator manifested a sudden increase of respect. "One moment, please."

Hockley heard the buzz and switch clicks of communication circuits reaching for the ship. Then, in a moment, he heard the somewhat irritated but familiar voice of his old friend.

"Waldon Thar speaking," the voice said. "Who wishes to talk?"

"Listen, you old son of a cyclotron's maiden aunt!" said Hockley. "Who would want to talk on Sol III? Why didn't you give me a buzz when you landed? I just found out you were here."

"Sherm Hockley, of course," the voice said with distant, unperturbed tones. "This is indeed a surprise and a pleasure. To be honest, I had forgotten Earth was your home planet."

"I'll try to think of something to jog your memory next time. How about getting together?"

"Well—I don't have very long," said Thar hesitantly. "If you could come over for a few minutes—"

Hockley had the jolting feeling that Waldon Thar would just as soon pass up the opportunity for their meeting. Some of the enthusiasm went out of his voice. "There's a good all-night interplanetary eatery and bar on the field there. I'll be along in fifteen minutes."

"Fine," said Thar, "but please try not to be late."

On the way to the field, Hockley wondered about the change that had apparently taken place in Thar. Of course, he had changed, too—perhaps for much the worse. But Thar sounded like a stuffed shirt now, and that is the last thing Hockley would have expected. In school, Thar had been the most irreverent of the whole class of irreverents, denouncing in ecstasy the established and unproven lore, riding the professors of unsubstantiated hypotheses. Now—well, he didn't sound like the Thar Hockley knew.

He took a table and sat down just as Thar entered the dining room. The latter's broad smile momentarily removed Hockley's doubts. The smile hadn't changed. And there was the same expression of devilish disregard for the established order. The same warm friendliness. It baffled Hockley to understand how Thar could have failed to remember Earth was his home.

Thar mentioned it as he came up and took Hockley's hand. "I'm terribly sorry," he said. "It was stupid to forget that Earth meant Sherman Hockley."

"I know how it is. I should have written. I guess I'm the one who owes a letter."

"No, I think not," said Thar.

They sat on opposite sides of a small table near a window and ordered drinks. On the field they could see the vast, shadowy outline of the Ryke vessel.

Thar was of a race genetically close to the Rykes. He lacked the feathery covering, but this was replaced by a layer of thin scales, which had a tendency to stand on edge when he was excited. He also wore a breathing piece, and carried the small shoulder tank with a faint air of superiority.

Hockley watched him with a growing sense of loss. The first impression had been more nearly correct. Thar hadn't wanted to meet him.

"It's been a long time," said Hockley lamely. "I guess there isn't much we did back there that means anything now."

"You shouldn't say that," said Thar as if recognizing he had been too remote. "Every hour of our acquaintance meant a great deal to me. I'll never forgive myself for forgetting—but tell me how you learned I was aboard the Ryke ship."

"The Rykes have made us an offer. I wanted to find out the effects on worlds that had accepted. I learned Janisson VIII was one, so I started looking."

"I'm so very glad you did, Sherm. You want me to confirm, of course, the advisability of accepting the offer Liacan has made."

"Confirm—or deny it," said Hockley.

Thar spread his clawlike hands. "Deny it? The most glorious opportunity a planet could possibly have?"

Something in Thar's voice gave Hockley a sudden chill. "How has it worked on your own world?"

"Janisson VIII has turned from a slum to a world of mansions. Our economic problems have been solved. Health and long life are routine. There is nothing we want that we cannot have for the asking."

"But are you satisfied with it? Is there nothing which you had to give up that you would like returned?"

Waldon Thar threw back his head and laughed in high pitched tones. "I might have known that would be the question you would ask! Forgive me, friend Sherman, but I had almost forgotten how unventuresome you are.

"Your question is ridiculous. Why should we wish to go back to our economic inequalities, poverty and distress, our ignorant plodding research in science? You can answer your own question."

They were silent for a moment. Hockley thought his friend would have gladly terminated their visit right there and returned to his ship. To forestall this, he leaned across the table and asked, "Your science—what has become of that?"

"Our science! We never had any. We were ignorant children playing with mud and rocks. We knew nothing. We had nothing. Until the Rykes offered to educate us."

"Surely you don't believe that," said Hockley quietly. "The problem you worked on at the Institute—gravity at microcosmic levels. That was not a childish thing."

Thar laughed shortly and bitterly. "What disillusionment you have coming, friend Sherman! If you only knew how truly childish it was. Wait until you learn from the Rykes the true conception of gravity, its nature and the part it plays in the structure of matter."

Hockley felt a sick tightening within him. This was not the Waldon Thar, the wild demon who thrust aside all authority and rumor in his own headlong search for knowledge. It couldn't be Thar who was sitting passively by, being told what the nature of the Universe is.

"Your scientists—?" Hockley persisted. "What has become of all your researchers?"

"The answer is the same," said Thar. "We had no science. We had no scientists. Those who once went by that name have become for the first time honest students knowing the pleasure of studying at the feet of masters."

"You have set up laboratories in which your researches are supervised by the Rykes?"

"Laboratories? We have no need of laboratories. We have workshops and study rooms where we try to absorb that which the Rykes discovered long ago. Maybe at some future time we will come to a point where we can reach into the frontier of knowledge with our own minds, but this does not seem likely now."

"So you have given up all original research of your own?"

"How could we do otherwise? The Rykes have all the answers to any question we have intelligence enough to ask. Follow them, Sherman. It is no disgrace to be led by such as the Ryke teachers."

"Don't you ever long," said Hockley, "to take just one short step on your own two feet?"

"Why crawl when you can go by trans-light carrier?"

Thar sipped the last of his drink and glanced toward the wall clock. "I must go. I can understand the direction of your questions and your thinking. You hesitate because you might lose the chance to play in the mud and count the pretty pebbles in the sand. Put away childish things. You will never miss them!"

They shook hands, and a moment later Hockley said goodbye to Thar at the entrance to the field. "I know Earth will accept," said Thar. "And you and I should not have lost contact—but we'll make up for it."

Watching him move toward the dark hulk of the ship, Hockley wondered if Thar actually believed that. In less than an hour they had exhausted all they had to say after twenty years. Hockley had the information he needed about the Ryke plan, but he wished he could have kept his old memories of his student friend. Thar was drunk on the heady stuff being peddled by the Rykes, and if what he said were true, it was strong enough to intoxicate a whole planet.

His blood grew cold at the thought. This was more than a fight for the National Laboratories. It was a struggle to keep all Mankind from becoming what Thar had become.

If he could have put Thar on exhibition in the meeting tomorrow, and shown what he was once like, he would have made his point. But Thar, before and after, was not available for exhibit. He had to find another way to show his colleagues and the Senators what the Rykes would make of them.

He glanced at his watch. They wouldn't like being wakened at this hour, but neither would the scientists put up much resistance to his request for support in Markham's meeting. He went back to the bar and called each of his colleagues who had been in the meeting that day.

Hockley was called first when the assembly convened at ten that morning. He rose slowly from his seat near Markham and glanced over the somewhat puzzled expressions of the scientists.

"I don't know that I can speak for the entire group of scientists present," he said. "We met yesterday and found some differences of opinion concerning this offer. While it is true there is overwhelming sentiment supporting it, certain questions remain, which we feel require additional data in order to be answered properly.

"While we recognize that official acceptance can be given to the Rykes with no approval whatever from the scientists, it seems only fair that we should have every opportunity to make what we consider a proper study and to express our opinions in the matter.

"To the non-scientist—and perhaps to many of my colleagues—it may seem inconceivable that there could be any questions whatever. But we wonder about the position of students of future generations, we wonder about the details of administration of the program, we wonder about the total effects of the program upon our society as a whole. We wish to ask permission to make further study of the matter in an effort to answer these questions and many others. We request permission to go as a committee to Rykeman III and make a first hand study of what the Rykes propose to do, how they will teach us, and how they will dispense the information they so generously offer.

"I ask that you consider this most seriously, and make an official request of the Rykes to grant us such opportunity for study, that you provide the necessary appropriations for the trip. I consider it most urgent that this be done at once."

There was a stir of concern and disapproval from Congressional members as Hockley sat down. Senators leaned to speak in whispers to their neighbors, but Hockley observed the scientists remained quiet and impassive. He believed he had sold them in his telephone calls during the early morning. They liked the idea of obtaining additional data. Besides, most of them wanted to see Rykeman III for themselves.

Senator Markham finally stood up, obviously disturbed by Hockley's abrupt proposal. "It has seemed to us members of the Committee that there could hardly be any need for more data than is already available to us. The remarkable effects of Ryke science on other backward worlds is common knowledge.

"On the other hand we recognize the qualifications of you gentlemen which make your request appear justified. We will have to discuss this at length, but at the moment I believe I can say I am in sympathy with your request and can encourage my Committee to give it serious consideration."

A great deal more was said on that and subsequent days. News of the Ryke offer was not given to the public, but the landing of the Ryke ship could not be hidden. It became known that Liacan carried his offer to other worlds and speculation was made that he offered it to Earth also. Angry questions were raised as to why the purpose of the visit was not clarified, but government silence was maintained while Hockley's request was considered.

It encountered bitter debate in the closed sessions, but permission was finally given for a junket of ninety scientists and ten senators to Rykeman III.

This could not be hidden, so the facts were modified and a story given out that the party was going to request participation in the Ryke program being offered other worlds, that Liacan's visit had not been conclusive.

In the days preceding the take-off Hockley felt a sense of destiny weighing heavily upon him. He read every word of the stream of opinion that flowed through the press. Every commentator and columnist seemed called upon to make his own specific analysis of the possibilities of the visit to Rykeman III. And the opinions were almost uniform that it would be an approach to

Utopia to have the Rykes take over. Hockley was sickened by this mass conversion to the siren call of the Rykes.

It was a tremendous relief when the day finally came and the huge transport ship lifted solemnly into space.

Most of the group were in the ship's lounge watching the television port as the Earth drifted away beneath them. Senator Markham seemed nervous and almost frightened, Hockley thought, as if something intangible had escaped him.

"I hope we're not wasting our time," he said. "Not that I don't understand your position," he added hastily to cover the show of antagonism he sensed creeping into his voice.

"We appreciate your support," said Hockley, "and we'll do our best to see the time of the investigation is not wasted."

But afterwards, when the two of them were alone by the screen, Silvers spoke to Hockley soberly. The mathematician had lost some of the wild exuberance he'd had at first. It had been replaced by a deep, intense conviction that nothing must stand in the way of Earth's alliance with the Rykes.

"We all understand why you wanted us to come," he said. "We know you believe this delay will cool our enthusiasm. It's only fair to make clear that it won't. How you intend to change us by taking us to the home of the Rykes has got us all baffled. The reverse will be true, I am very sure. We intend to make it clear to the Rykes that we accept their offer. I hope you have no plan to make a declaration to the contrary."

Hockley kept his eyes on the screen, watching the green sphere of Earth. "I have no intention of making any statement of any kind. I was perfectly honest when I said our understanding of the Rykes would profit by this visit. You all agreed. I meant nothing more nor less than what I said. I hope no one in the group thinks otherwise."

"We don't know," said Silvers.

"It's just that you've got us wondering how you expect to change our views."

"I have not said that is my intention."

"Can you say it is not?"

"No, I cannot say that. But the question is incomplete. My whole intention is to discover as fully as possible what will be the result of alliance with the Rykes. If you should conclude that it will be unfavorable that will be the result of your own direct observations and computations, not of my arguments."

"You may be sure that is one thing that will not occur," said Silvers.

It took them a month to reach a transfer point where they could change to a commercial vessel using Ryke principles. In the following week they covered a distance several thousand times that which they had already come. And then they were on Rykeman III.

A few of them had visited the planet previously, on vacation trips or routine study expeditions, but most of them were seeing it for the first time. While well out into space the group began crowding the vision screens which brought into range the streets and buildings of the cities. They could see the people walking and riding there.

Hockley caught his breath at the sight, and doubts overwhelmed him, telling him he was an utter and complete fool. The city upon which he looked was a jewel of perfection. Buildings were not indiscriminate masses of masonry and metal and plastic heaped up without regard to the total effect. Rather, the city was a unit created with an eye to esthetic perfection.

Silvers stood beside Hockley. "We've got a chance to make Earth look that way," said the mathematician.

"There's only one thing missing," said Hockley. "The price tag. We still need to know what it's going to cost."

Upon landing, the Earthmen were greeted by a covey of their bird-like hosts who scurried about, introducing themselves in their high whistling voices. In busses, they were moved half way across the city to a building which stood beside an enormous park area.

It was obviously a building designed for the reception of just such delegations as this one, giving Hockley evidence that perhaps his idea was not so original after all. It was a relief to get inside after their brief trip across the city. Gravity, temperature, and air pressure and composition duplicated those of Earth inside, and conditions could be varied to accommodate many different species. Hockley felt confident they could become accustomed to outside conditions after a few days, but it was exhausting now to be out for long.

They were shown to individual quarters and given leisure to unpack and inspect their surroundings. Furniture had been adjusted to their size and needs. The only oversight Hockley could find was a faint odor of chlorine lingering in the closets. He wondered who the last occupant of the room had been.

After a noon meal, served with foods of astonishingly close approximation to their native fare, the group was offered a prelude to the general instruction and indoctrination which would begin the following day. This was in the form of a guided tour through the science museum which, Hockley gathered, was a modernized Ryke parallel to the venerable Smithsonian back home. The tour was entirely optional, as far as the planned program of the Rykes was concerned, but none of the Earthmen turned it down.

Hockley tried to concentrate heavily on the memory of Waldon Thar and keep the image of his friend always before him as he moved through the city and inspected the works of the Rykes. He found it helped suppress the awe and adulation which he had an impulse to share with his companions.

It was possible even, he found, to adopt a kind of truculent cynicism toward the approach the Rykes were making. The visit to the science museum could be an attempt to bowl them over with an eon-long vista of Ryke superiority in the sciences. At least that was most certainly the effect on them. Hockley cursed his own feeling of ignorance and inferiority as the guide led them quietly past the works of the masters, offering but little comment, letting them see for themselves the obvious relationships.

In the massive display showing developments of spaceflight, the atomic vessels, not much different from Earthmen's best efforts, were far down the line, very near to the earliest attempts of the Rykes to rocket their way into space. Beyond that level was an incredible series of developments incomprehensible to most of the Earthmen.

And to all their questions the guide offered the monotonous reply: "That will be explained to you later. We only wish to give you an overall picture of our culture at the present time."

But this was not enough for one of the astronomers, named Moore, who moved ahead of Hockley in the crowd. Hockley saw the back of Moore's neck growing redder by the minute as the guide's evasive answer was repeated. Finally, Moore forced a discussion regarding the merits of some systems of comparing the brightness of stars, which the guide briefly showed them. The guide, in great annoyance, burst out with a stream of explanation that completely flattened any opinions Moore might have had. But at the same time the astronomer grinned amiably at the Ryke. "That ought to settle that," he said. "I'll bet it won't take a week to get our system changed back home."

Moore's success loosened the restraint of the others and they beseiged the guide mercilessly then with opinions, questions, comparisons—and even mild disapprovals. The guide's exasperation was obvious—and pleasant—to Hockley, who remained a bystander. It was frightening to Markham and some of the other senators who were unable to take part in the discussion. But most of the scientists failed to notice it in their eagerness to learn.

After dinner that night they gathered in the lounge and study of their quarters. Markham stood beside Hockley as they partook cautiously of the cocktails which the Rykes had attempted to duplicate for them. The Senator's awe had returned to overshadow any concern he felt during the events of the afternoon. "A wonderful day!" he said. "Even though this visit delays completion of our arrangements with the Rykes those of us here will be grateful forever that you proposed it. Nothing could have so impressed us all with the desirability of accepting the Ryke's tutelage. It was a stroke of genius, Dr. Hockley. And for a time I thought you were actually opposed to the Rykes!"

He sipped his drink while Hockley said nothing. Then his brow furrowed a bit. "But I wonder why our guide cut short our tour this afternoon. If I recall correctly he said at the beginning there was a great deal more to see than he actually showed us."

Hockley smiled and sipped politely at his drink before he set it down and faced the Senator. "I was wondering if anyone else noticed that," he said.

Hockley slept well that night except for the fact that occasional whiffs of chlorine seemed to drift from various corners of the room even though he turned the air-conditioning system on full blast.

In the morning there began a series of specialized lectures which had been prepared in accordance with the Earthmen's request to acquaint them with what they would be getting upon acceptance of the Ryke offer.

It was obviously no new experience for the Rykes. The lectures were well prepared and anticipated many questions. The only thing new about it, Hockley thought, was the delivery in the language of the Earthmen. Otherwise, he felt this was something prepared a long time ago and given a thousand times or more.

They were divided into smaller groups according to their specialties, electronic men going one way, astronomers and mathematical physicists another, chemists and general physicists in still another direction. Hockley, Showalter and the senators were considered more or less free floating members of the delegation with the privilege of visiting with one group or another according to their pleasure.

Hockley chose to spend the first day with the chemists, since that was his own first love. Dr. Showalter and Senator Markham came along with him. As much as he tried he found it virtually impossible not to sit with the same open-mouthed wonder that his colleagues exhibited. The swift, free-flowing exposition of the Ryke lecturer led them immediately beyond their own realms, but so carefully did he lead them that it seemed that they must have come this way before, and forgotten it.

Hockley felt half angry with himself. He felt he had allowed himself to be hypnotized by the skill of the Ryke, and wondered despairingly if there were any chance at all of combating their approach. He saw nothing to indicate it in the experience of that day or the ones immediately following. But he retained hope that there was much significance in the action of the guide who had cut short their visit to the museum.

In the evenings, in the study lounge of the dormitory, they held interminable bull sessions exchanging and digesting what they had been shown during the day. It was at the end of the third day that Hockley thought he could detect a subtle change in the group. He had some difficulty analyzing it at first. It seemed to be a growing aliveness, a sort of recovery. And then he recognized that the initial stunned reaction to the magnificence of the Rykes was passing off. They had been shocked by the impact of the Rykes, almost as if they had been struck a blow on the head. Temporarily, they had shelved all their own analytical and critical facilities and yielded to the Rykes without question.

Now they were beginning to recover, springing back to a condition considerably nearer normal. Hockley felt a surge of encouragement as he detected a more sharply critical evaluation in the conversations that buzzed around him. The enthusiasm was more measured.

It was the following evening, however, that witnessed the first event of pronounced shifting of anyone's attitude. They had finished dinner and were gathering in the lounge, sparring around, setting up groups for the bull sessions that would go until long after midnight. Most of them had already settled down and were talking part in conversations or were listening quietly when they were suddenly aware of a change in the atmosphere of the room.

For a moment there was a general turning of heads to locate the source of the disturbance. Hockley knew he could never describe just what made him look around, but he was abruptly conscious that Dr. Silvers was walking into the lounge and looking slowly about at those gathered there. Something in his presence was like the sudden appearance of a thundercloud, his face seemed to reflect the dark turbulence of a summer storm.

He said nothing, however, to anyone but strode over and sat beside Hockley, who was alone at the moment smoking the next to last of his Earthside cigars. Hockley felt the smouldering turmoil inside the mathematician. He extended his final cigar. Silvers brushed it away.

"The last one," said Hockley mildly. "In spite of all their abilities the Ryke imitations are somewhat less than natural."

Silvers turned slowly to face Hockley. "I presented them with the Legrandian Equations today," he said. "I expected to get a straightforward answer to a perfectly legitimate scientific question. That is what we were led to expect, was it not?"

Hockley nodded. "That's my impression. Did you get something less than a straightforward answer?"

The mathematician exhaled noisily. "The Legrandian Equations will lead to a geometry as revolutionary as Riemann's was in his day. But I was told by the Rykes that I 'should dismiss it from all further consideration. It does not lead to any profitable mathematical development.'"

Hockley felt that his heart most certainly skipped a beat, but he managed to keep his voice steady, and sympathetic. "That's too bad. I know what high hopes you had. I suppose you will give up work on the Equations now?"

"I will not!" Silvers exclaimed loudly. Nearby groups who had returned hesitantly to their own conversations now stared at him again. But abruptly he changed his tone and looked almost pleadingly at Hockley. "I don't understand it. Why should they say such a thing? It appears to be one of the most profitable avenues of exploration I have encountered in my whole career. And the Rykes brush it aside!"

"What did you say when they told you to give it up?"

"I said I wanted to know where the development would lead. I said it had been indicated that we could have an answer to any scientific problem within the range of their abilities, and certainly this is, from what I've seen.

"The instructor replied that I'd been given an answer to my question, that 'the first lesson you must learn if you wish to acquire our pace in science is to recognize that we have been along the path ahead of you. We know which are the possibilities that are worthwhile to develop. We have gained our speed by learning to bypass every avenue but the main one, and not get lost in tempting side roads.'

"He said that we've got to learn to trust them and take their word as to which is the correct and profitable field of research, that 'we will show you where to go, as we agreed to do. If you are not willing to accept our leadership in this respect our agreement means nothing.' Wouldn't that be a magnificent way to make scientific progress!"

The mathematician shifted in his chair as if trying to control an internal fury that would not be capped. He held out his hand abruptly. "I'll take that cigar after all, if you don't mind, Hockley."

With savage energy he chewed the end and ignited the cigar, then blew a mammoth cloud of smoke ceilingward. "I think the trouble must be in our lecturer," he said. "He's crazy. He couldn't possibly represent the conventional attitude of the Rykes. They promised to give answers to our problems—and this is the kind of nonsense I get. I'm going to see somebody higher up and find out why we can't have a lecturer who knows what he's talking about. Or maybe you or Markham would rather take it up—through official channels, as it were?"

"The Ryke was correct," said Hockley. "He did give you an answer."

"He could answer all our questions that way!"

"You're perfectly right," said Hockley soberly. "He could do exactly that."

"They won't of course," said Silvers, defensively. "Even if this particular character isn't just playing the screwball, my question is just a special case. It's just one particular thing they consider to be valueless. Perhaps in the end I'll find they're right—but I'm going to develop a solution to these Equations if it takes the rest of my life!

"After all, they admit they have no solution, that they have not bothered to go down this particular side path, as they put it. If we don't go down it how can we ever know whether it's worthwhile or not? How can the Rykes know what they may have missed by not doing so?"

"I can't answer that," said Hockley. "For us or for them, I know of no other way to predict the outcome of a specific line of research except to carry it through and find out what lies at the end of the road."

Hockley didn't sleep very well after he finally went to bed that night. Silvers had presented him with the break he had been expecting and hoping for. The first chink in the armor of sanctity surrounding the Rykes. Now he wondered what would follow, if this would build up to the impassable barrier he wanted, or if it would merely remain a sore obstacle in their way but eventually be bypassed and forgotten.

He did not believe it would be the only incident of its kind. There would be others as the Earthmen's stunned, blind acceptance gave way completely to sound, critical evaluation. And in any case there was one delegate who would never be the same again. No matter how he eventually rationalized it Dr. Forman K. Silvers would never feel quite the same about the Rykes as he did before they rejected his favorite piece of research.

Hockley arose early, eager but cautious, his senses open for further evidence of disaffection springing up. He joined the group of chemists once more for the morning lecture. The spirit of the group was markedly higher than when he first met with them. They had been inspired by what the Rykes had shown them, but in addition their own sense of judgment had been brought out of suspension.

The Ryke lecturer began inscribing on the board an enormous organic formula, using conventions of Earth chemistry for the benefit of his audience. He explained at some length a number of transformations which it was possible to make in the compound by means of high intensity fields.

Almost at once, one of the younger chemists named Dr. Carmen, was on his feet exclaiming excitedly that one of the transformation compounds was a chemical on which he had conducted an extensive research. He had produced enough to know that it had a multitude of intriguing properties, and now he was exuberant at the revelation of a method of producing it in quantity and also further transforming it.

At his sudden enthusiasm the lecturer's face took on what they had come to recognize as a very dour look. "That series of transformations has no interest for us," he said. "I merely indicated its existence to show one of the possibilities which should be avoided. Over here you see the direction in which we wish to go."

"But you never saw anything with properties like that!" Carmen protested. "It goes through an incredible series of at least three crystalline-liquid phase changes with an increase in pressure alone. But with proper control of heat it can be kept in the crystalline phase regardless of pressure. It is closely related to a drug series with anesthetic properties, and is almost sure to be valuable in—"

The Ryke lecturer cut him off sharply. "I have explained," he said, "the direction of transformation in which we are interested. Your concern is not with anything beyond the boundaries which our study has proven to be the direct path of research and study."

"Then I should abandon research on this series of chemicals?" Carmen asked with a show of outward meekness.

The Ryke nodded with pleasure at Carmen's submissiveness.

"That is it precisely. We have been over this ground long ago. We know where the areas of profitable study lie. You will be told what to observe and what to ignore. How could you ever hope to make progress if you stopped to examine every alternate probability and possibility that appeared to you?" He shook his head vigorously and his plume vibrated with emotion.

"You must have a plan," he continued. "A goal. Study of the Universe cannot proceed in any random, erratic fashion. You must know what you want and then find out where to look for it."

Carmen sat down slowly. Hockley was sure the Ryke did not notice the tense bulge of the chemist's jaw muscles. Perhaps he would not have understood the significance if he had noticed.

Hockley was a trifle late in getting to the dining room at lunch time that day. By the time he did so the place was like a beehive. He was almost repelled by the furor of conversation circulating in the room as he entered.

He passed through slowly, searching for a table of his own. He paused a moment behind Dr. Carmen, who was declaiming in no mild terms his opinions of a system that would pre-select those areas of research which were to be entered and those which were not. He smiled a little as he caught the eye of one of the dozen chemists seated at the table, listening.

Moving on, he observed that Silvers had also cornered a half dozen or so of his colleagues in his own field and was in earnest conversation with them—in a considerably more restrained manner, however, than he had used the previous evening with Hockley, or than Carmen was using at the present time.

The entire room was abuzz with similar groups.

The senators had tried to mingle with the others in past days, always with more or less lack of success because they found themselves out of the conversation almost completely. Today they had no luck whatever. They were seated together at a couple of tables in a corner. None of them seemed to be paying attention to the food before them, but were glancing about, half-apprehensively, at their fellow diners—who were also paying no attention to food.

Hockley caught sight of his political colleagues and sensed their dismay. The field of disquietude seemed almost tangible in the air. The senators seemed half frightened by what they felt but could not understand.

Showalter's wild waving at the far corner of the room finally caught Hockley's eye and he moved toward the small table which the assistant had reserved for them. Showalter was upset, too, by the atmosphere within the room.

"What the devil is up?" he said. "Seems like everybody's on edge this morning. I never saw a bunch of guys so touchy. You'd think they woke up with snakes in their beds."

"Didn't you know?" said Hockley. "Haven't you been to any of the lectures this morning?"

"No. A couple of the senators were getting bored with all the scientific doings so I thought maybe I should try to entertain

105

them. We took in what passes for such here, but it wasn't much better than the lectures as a show. Tell me what's up."

Briefly, Hockley described Silvers' upset of the day before and Carmen's experience that morning. Showalter let his glance rove over his fellow Earthmen, trying to catch snatches of the buzzing conversation at nearby tables.

"You think that's the kind of thing that's got them all going this morning?" he said.

Hockley nodded. "I caught enough of it passing through to know that's what it is. I gather that every group has run into the same kind of thing by now, the fencing off of broad areas where we have already tried to do research.

"After the first cloud of awe wore off, the first thing everyone wanted was an answer to his own pet line of research. Nine times out of ten it was something the Rykes told them to chuck down the drain. That advice doesn't sit so well—as you can plainly see."

Showalter drew back his gaze and stared for a long time at Hockley. "You knew this would happen. That's why you brought us here—"

"I had hopes of it. I was reasonably sure this was the way the Rykes operated."

Showalter remained thoughtful for a long time before he spoke again. "You've won your point, I suppose, as far as this group goes, but you can't hope to convince all of Earth by this. The

Rykes will hold their offer open, and others will accept it on behalf of Earth.

"And what if it's we who are wrong, in the end? How can you be sure that this isn't the way the Rykes have made their tremendous speed—by not going down all the blind alleys that we rattle around in."

"I'm sure it is the way they have attained such speed of advancement."

"Then maybe we ought to go along, regardless of our own desires. Maybe we never did know how to do research!"

Hockley smiled across the table at his assistant. "You believe that, of course."

"I'm just talking," said Showalter irritably. "The thing gets more loopy every day. If you think you understand the Rykes I wish you would give out with what the score is. By the looks of most of these guys I would say they are getting ready to throttle the next Ryke they see instead of knuckle under to him."

"I hope you're right," said Hockley fervently. "I certainly hope you're right."

By evening there was increasing evidence that he was. Hockley passed up the afternoon lecture period and spent the time in the lounge doing some thinking of his own. He knew he couldn't push the group. Above all, he mustn't give way to any temptation to push them or say, "I told you so." Their present frustration was so deep that their antagonism could be turned almost indiscriminately in any direction, and he would be offering himself as a ready target if he were not careful.

On the other hand he had to be ready to take advantage of their disaffection and throw them a decisive challenge when they were ready for it. That might be tonight, or it might be another week. He wished for a sure way of knowing. As things turned out, however, the necessity of choosing the time was taken from him.

After dinner that night, when the group began to drift into the lounge, Silvers and Carmen and three of the other men came over to where Hockley sat. Silvers fumbled with the buttons of his coat as if preparing to make an address.

"We'd like to request," he said, "that is—we think we ought to get together. We'd like you to call a meeting, Hockley. Some of us have a few things we'd like to talk over."

Hockley nodded, his face impassive.

"The matter I mentioned to you the other night," said Silvers. "It's been happening to all the men. We think we ought to talk about it."

"Fine," said Hockley. "I've been thinking it would perhaps be a good idea. Pass the word around and let's get some chairs. We can convene in ten minutes."

The others nodded somberly and moved away with all the enthusiasm of preparing for a funeral. And maybe that's what it would be, Hockley thought—somebody's funeral. He hoped it would be the Rykes.

The room began filling almost at once, as if they had been expecting the call. In little more than five minutes it seemed that every member of the Earth delegation had assembled, leaving time to spare.

The senators still wore their looks of puzzlement and half-frightened anxiety, which had intensified if anything. There was no puzzlement on the faces of the scientists, however, only a set and determined expression that Hockley hardly dared interpret as meaning they had made up their minds. He had to have their verbal confirmation.

Informally, he thrust his hands in his pockets and sauntered to the front of the group.

"I have been asked to call a meeting," he said, "by certain members of the group who have something on their minds. They seem to feel we'd all be interested in what is troubling them. Since I have nothing in particular to say I'm simply going to turn the floor over to those of you who have. Dr. Silvers first approached me to call this discussion, so I shall ask him to lead off. Will you come to the front, Dr. Silvers?"

The mathematician rose as if wishing someone else would do the talking. He stood at one side of the group, halfway to the rear. "I can do all right from here," he said.

After a pause, as if coming to a momentous decision, he plunged into his complaint. "It appears that nearly all of us have encountered an aspect of the Ryke culture and character which was not anticipated when we first received their offer." Briefly, he related the details of the Ryke rejection of his research on the Legrandian Equations.

"We were told we were going to have all our questions

answered, that the Ryke's science included all we could anticipate or hope to accomplish in the next few millenia. I swallowed that. We all did. It appears we were slightly in error. It begins to appear as if we are not going to find the intellectual paradise we anticipated."

He smiled wryly. "I'm sure none of you is more ready than I to admit he has been a fool. It appears that paradise, so-called, consists merely of a few selected gems which the Rykes consider particularly valuable, while the rest of the field goes untouched.

"I want to offer public apologies to Dr. Hockley, who saw and understood the situation as it actually existed, while the rest of us had our heads in the clouds. Exactly how he knew, I'm not sure, but he did, and very brilliantly chose the only way possible to convince us that what he knew was correct.

"I suggest we do our packing tonight, gentlemen. Let us return at once to our laboratories and spend the rest of our lives in some degree of atonement for being such fools as to fall for the line the Rykes tried to sell us."

Hockley's eyes were on the senators. At first there were white faces filled with incredulity as the mathematician proceeded. Then slowly this changed to sheer horror.

When Silvers finished, there was immediate bedlam. There was a clamor of voices from the scientists, most of whom seemed to be trying to affirm Silvers' position. This was offset by explosions of rage from the senatorial members of the group.

Hockley let it go, not even raising his hands for order until finally the racket died of its own accord as the eyes of the delegates came to rest upon him.

And then, before he could speak, Markham was on his feet. "This is absolutely moral treachery," he thundered. "I have never heard a more vicious revocation of a pledged word than I have heard this evening.

"You men are not alone concerned in this matter. For all practical purposes you are not concerned at all! And yet to take it upon yourselves to pass judgment in a matter that is the affair of the entire population of Earth—out of nothing more than sheer spite because the Rykes refuse recognition of your own childish projects! I have never heard a more incredible and infantile performance than you supposedly mature gentlemen of science are expressing this evening."

He glared defiantly at Hockley, who was again the center of attention moving carelessly to the center of the stage. "Anybody want to try to answer the Senator?" he asked casually.

Instantly, a score of men were on their feet, speaking simultaneously. They stopped abruptly, looking deferentially to their neighbors and at Hockley, inviting him to choose one of them to be spokesman.

"Maybe I ought to answer him myself," said Hockley, "since I predicted that this would occur, and that we ought to make a trial run before turning our collective gray matter over to the Rykes."

A chorus of approval and nodding heads gave him the go ahead.

"The Senator is quite right in saying that we few are not alone in our concern in this matter," he said. "But the Senator intends to imply a major difference between us scientists and the rest of mankind. This is his error.

"Every member of Mankind who is concerned about the Universe in which he lives, is a scientist. You need to understand what a scientist is—and you can say no more than that he is a human being trying to solve the problem of understanding his Universe, immediate or remote. He is concerned about the inanimate worlds, his own personality, his fellow men—and the interweaving relationships among all these factors. We professional scientists are no strange species, alien to our race. Our only difference is perhaps that we undertake more problems than does the average of our fellow men, and of a more complex kind. That is all.

"The essence of our science is a relentless personal yearning to know and understand the Universe. And in that, the scientist must not be forbidden to ask whatever question occurs to him. The moment we put any restraint upon our fields of inquiry, or set bounds to the realms of our mental aspirations, our science ceases to exist and becomes a mere opportunist technology."

Markham stood up, his face red with exasperation and rage. "No one is trying to limit you! Why is that so unfathomable to your minds? You are being offered a boundless expanse, and you continue to make inane complaints of limitations. The Rykes have been over all the territory you insist on exploring. They can tell you the number of pretty pebbles and empty shells that lie there. You are like children insistent upon exploring every shadowy corner and peering behind every useless bush on a walk through the forest.

"Such is to be expected of a child, but not of an adult, who is capable of taking the word of one who has been there before!"

"There are two things wrong with your argument," said Hockley. "First of all, there is no essential difference between the learning of a child who must indeed explore the dark corners and strange growths by which he passes—there is no difference between this and the probing of the scientist, who must explore the Universe with his own senses and with his own instruments, without, taking another's word that there is nothing there worth seeing.

"Secondly, the Rykes themselves are badly in error in asserting that they have been along the way ahead of us. They have not. In all their fields of science they have limited themselves badly to one narrow field of probability. They have taken a narrow path stretching between magnificent vistas on either side of them, and have deliberately ignored all that was beyond the path and on the inviting side trails."

"Is there anything wrong with that?" demanded Markham. "If you undertake a journey you don't weave in and out of every possible path that leads in every direction opposed to your destination. You take the direct route. Or at least ordinary people do."

"Scientists do, too," said Hockley, "when they take a journey. Professional science is not a journey, however. It's an exploration.

"There is a great deal wrong with what the Rykes have done.

They have assumed, and would have us likewise assume, that there is a certain very specific future toward which we are all moving. This future is built out of the discoveries they have made about the Universe. It is made of the system of mathematics they have developed, which exclude Dr. Silvers' cherished Legrandian Equations. It excludes the world in which exist Dr. Carmen's series of unique compounds.

"The Rykes have built a wonderful, workable world of serenity, beauty, scientific consistency, and economic adjustment. They have eliminated enormous amounts of chaos which Earthmen continue to suffer.

"But we do not want what the Rykes have obtained—if we have to pay their price for it."

"Then you are complete fools," said Markham. "Fortunately, you cannot and will not speak for all of Earth."

Hockley paced back and forth a half dozen steps, his eyes on the floor. "I think we do—and can—speak for all our people," he said. "Remember, I said that all men are scientists in the final analysis. I am very certain that no Earthman who truly understood the situation would want to face the future which the Rykes hold out to us."

"And why not?" demanded Markham.

"Because there are too many possible futures. We refuse to march down a single narrow trail to the golden future. That's what the Rykes would have us do. But they are wrong. It would be like taking a trip through a galaxy at speeds faster than light—and claiming to have seen the galaxy. What the Rykes have obtained is genuine and good, but what they have not obtained is perhaps far better and of greater worth."

"How can you know such an absurd thing?"

"We can't—not for sure," said Hockley. "Not until we go there and see for ourselves, step by step. But we aren't going to be confined to the Rykes' narrow trail. We are going on a broad path to take in as many byways as we can possibly find. We'll explore every probability we come to, and look behind every bush and under every pebble.

"We will move together, the thousands and the millions of us, simultaneously, interacting with one another, exchanging data. Most certainly, many will end up in blind alleys. Some will find data that seems the ultimate truth at one point and pure deception at another. Who can tell ahead of time which of these multiple paths we should take? Certainly not the Rykes, who have bypassed most of them!

"It doesn't matter that many paths lead to failure—not as long as we remain in communication with each other. In the end we will find the best possible future for us. But there is no one future, only a multitude of possible futures. We must have the right to build the one that best fits our own kind."

"Is that more important than achieving immediately a more peaceful, unified, and secure society?" said Markham.

"Infinitely more important!" said Hockley.

"It is fortunate at least, then, that you are in no position to implement these insane beliefs of yours. The Ryke program was offered to Earth, and it shall be accepted on behalf of Earth. You may be sure of a very poor hearing when you try to present these notions back home."

"You jump to conclusions, Senator," said Hockley with mild confidence. "Why do you suppose I proposed this trip if I did not believe I could do something about the situation? I assure you that we did not come just to see the sights."

Markham's jaw slacked and his face became white. "What do you mean? You haven't dared to try to alienate the Rykes—"

"I mean that there is a great deal we can do about the situation. Now that the sentiments of my colleagues parallel my own I'm sure they agree that we must effectively and finally spike any possibility of Earth's becoming involved in this Ryke nonsense."

"You wouldn't dare!—even if you could—"

"We can, and we dare," said Hockley. "When we return to Earth we shall have to report that the Rykes have refused to admit Earth to their program. We shall report that we made every effort to obtain an agreement with them, but it was in vain. If anyone wishes to verify the report, the Rykes themselves will say that this is quite true: they cannot possibly consider Earth as a participant. If you contend that an offer was once made, you will not find the Rykes offering much support since they will be very busily denying that we are remotely qualified."

"The Rykes are hardly ones to meekly submit to any idiotic plan of that kind."

"They can't help it—if we demonstrate that we are quite unqualified to participate."

"You—you—"

"It will not be difficult," said Hockley. "The Rykes have set up a perfect teacher-pupil situation, with all the false assumptions that go with it. There is at least one absolutely positive way to disintegrate such a situation. The testimony of several thousand years' failure of our various educational systems indicates that there are quite a variety of lesser ways also—

"Perhaps you are aware of the experiences and techniques commonly employed on Earth by white men in their efforts to educate the aborigine. The first procedure is to do away with the tribal medicine men, ignore their lore and learning. Get them to give up the magic words and their pots of foul smelling liquids, abandon their ritual dances and take up the white man's great wisdom.

"We have done this time after time, only to learn decades later that the natives once knew much of anesthetics and healing drugs, and had genuine powers to communicate in ways the white man can't duplicate.

"But once in a long while a group of aborigines show more spunk than the average. They refuse to give up their medicine men, their magic and their hard earned lore accumulated over generations and centuries. Instead of giving these things up they insist on the white man's learning these mysteries in preference to his nonsensical and ineffective magic. They completely frustrate the situation, and if they persist they finally destroy the white man as an educator. He is forced to conclude that the ignorant savages are unteachable.

"It is an infallible technique—and one that we shall employ. Dr. Silvers will undertake to teach his mathematical lecturer in the approaches to the Legrandian Equations. He will speculate long and noisily on the geometry which potentially lies in this mathematical system. Dr. Carmen will elucidate at great length on the properties of the chain of chemicals he has been advised to abandon.

"Each of us has at least one line of research the Rykes would have us give up. That is the very thing we shall insist on having investigated. We shall teach them these things and prove Earthmen to be an unlearned, unteachable band of aborigines who refuse to pursue the single path to glory and light, but insist on following every devious byway and searching every darkness that lies beside the path.

"It ought to do the trick. I estimate it should not be more than a week before we are on our way back home, labeled by the Rykes as utterly hopeless material for their enlightenment."

The senators seemed momentarily appalled and speechless, but they recovered shortly and had a considerable amount of high flown oratory to distribute on the subject. The scientists, however, were comparatively quiet, but on their faces was a subdued glee that Hockley had to admit was little short of fiendish. It was composed, he thought, of all the gloating anticipations of all the schoolboys who had ever put a thumbtack on the teacher's chair.

Hockley was somewhat off in his prediction. It was actually a mere five days after the beginning of the Earthmen's campaign that the Rykes gave them up and put them firmly aboard a vessel bound for home. The Rykes were apologetic but firm in admitting they had made a sorry mistake, that Earthmen would have to go their own hopeless way while the Rykes led the rest of the Universe toward enlightenment and glory.

Hockley, Showalter, and Silvers watched the planet drop away beneath them. Hockley could not help feeling sympathetic toward the Rykes. "I wonder what will happen," he said slowly, "when they crash headlong into an impassable barrier on that beautiful, straight road of theirs. I wonder if they'll ever have enough guts to turn aside?"

"I doubt it," said Showalter. "They'll probably curl up and call it a day."

Silvers shook his head as if to ward off an oppressive vision. "That shouldn't be allowed to happen," he said. "They've got too much. They've achieved too much, in spite of their limitations. I wonder if there isn't some way we could help them?"

THE END